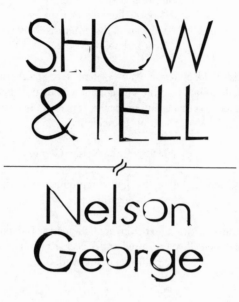

SHOW & TELL

Nelson George

Published by Simon and Schuster

NEW YORK LONDON TORONTO SYDNEY SINGAPORE

Simon & Schuster, Inc.
Rockefeller Center
1230 Avenue of the Americas
New York, NY 10020

SCRIBNER FICTION and design are trademarks of Macmillan Library Reference USA, Inc., used under license by Simon & Schuster, the publisher of this work.

Designed by Colin Joh
Text set in Electra

Manufactured in the United States of America

ISBN 0-7394-1692-8

To Chester Himes.
For giving me the freedom.

SeeCee:

I invite you to come dream with me. If you open up to me I will not hurt you. I will not lie to you. I will be who I really am. I will touch you in that space no one has before and my hands will be soft. My hands will be familiar. That's because my hands will be your hands. I will facilitate for you. I will give you entry to things you haven't seen before and, in so doing, allow you to see sides of yourself you've been hiding. That's a promise. So come join me in a private room, but only if you can handle this much intimacy.

You feel me?

Chapter 1

To all the world, we looked like what we were—two well-groomed black urban professionals sharing a quiet drink, maybe talking shop. But the observant barfly at the Rhiga Royal bar would have noticed the fine brown lady's well-stocked Prada travel bag and the way I—the guy with the salt-and-pepper beard and the beige gabardine suit—anxiously fingered the key to suite 3003.

This was no casual encounter. No improvised meeting. I'd been planning this night for a month, ever since Mildred "Millie" Jackson had announced that she'd be hitting the road for about a month to visit current clients and potential new investments. Before her journey I wanted us to have a magical New York weekend, the kind tourists save up for and we residents are always too busy to plan. A weekend to give the girl some masturbation-inspiring memories for those long (hopefully), lonely nights across America.

Up in the living room of 3003 there were the three dozen roses I'd ordered and the chilled champagne I'd requested. But before Millie could touch one rose or take one sip, I made her open the mirrored double doors to the boudoir.

"What's in there, Dean?" she asked in a happily nervous voice.

"Something that will melt in your mouth," I told her.

This made Millie very giddy and she swung open the doors with a vicious glee. She walked right up to the cream-colored king-size bed and looked down at what I'd left there.

Sitting on a pillow in the center of the bed was a box of Godiva chocolates the same dark mocha tone as her skin. Millie wondered aloud, "Are these for me?" and then picked up the box.

I came up behind her, my hands gripping the sides of her hips tightly as a drowning man grips a life raft. I pressed my pants against the back of her beige skirt and whispered, "No. They're for us."

"But," she purred in protest, "it's my birthday."

"Yeah," I countered, biting her neck, "but it's my party." She tried to turn around and face me, but I held her hips in check and pulled off her jacket with my teeth.

Don't actually know how I managed that, but when I was through, her blue jacket lay next to her black sling-backs and my brown loafers on the thick cream carpet. Soon after, the jacket was joined by her silk blouse, my cotton shirt, her black bra, my gabardine suit jacket and the top of the Godiva box. Millie sat on the edge of the bed and faced me. I looked up at her from my knees.

At age thirty-seven Millie showed only faint traces of encroaching middle age. Her belly was definitely rounder than she'd like and, if she got too preoccupied with work, a wrinkle line might crease her forehead. Other than that, Millie had it going on. Her legs—Millie's pride and joy—were strong, taut and as shapely as a nineteen-year-old gymnast's. They were at the center of her sexual self-confidence and the tool she used, so expertly, to woo. At our first lunch date, Millie swung them around, back and forth. I spent our lunch ignoring my steak, instead savoring the idea of nibbling the backs of her legs from ankle to ass. On this day that marked her thirty-seventh year on earth, I was doing that and so much more.

To the joy of my dentist and the delight of my Millie, I was using the Godiva chocolates as a kind of lotion. I sucked on a large chunk of mocha, then leaned over and painted Millie's small, soft breasts with a loving coat of brown sugar. Then I slowly rubbed the saliva-lubricated chocolates up, down and across my woman's body until her skin was crisscrossed with sweet streaks my tongue was then obliged to erase.

Licking a woman's body clean of Godiva chocolate is not a job for an impatient man. To do it right one definitely needs several sweet teeth and an appetite for mocha (and caramel and hazelnut) and a woman who likes to be stirred before she is shaken, all of which I happily possessed.

Before long the brown streaks on Millie's torso had been replaced with long, wet lines of my sweat and spit. With that pleasant task completed, I slipped a beige hunk of caramel between my lips and headed downtown. Millie's agile legs curled around my head and led me down to her favorite spot. Millie's head fell back and she let out a low, throaty moan, while I rolled the caramel in a small circle around the opening to her red, grateful pussy.

Millie used those firm, solid legs to control me, squeezing my head tighter when she wanted to go faster, loosening when she wanted to go slower. By the time the caramel had disappeared from my lips, the outlines of my ears were etched on the inside of her thighs. Millie slid back onto the bed, her vulva shiny and beckoning me to visit. From my pants I liberated a green and white pack of Trojan lubricated extra-large condoms and smiled. I let Millie see it and then glanced at the digital clock at the head of the bed.

"Sweetness," I said softly, "it's six forty-five. I don't think we have time."

"It won't take that long, baby," she said, touching my penis with her toes. I reluctantly slipped out of her grip.

"Come on, Millie," I replied, "you know how we do."

"You're not right, Dean," she said.

"Patience is a frustrating damn virtue," I said, pulling Millie from the bed and guiding her into the bathroom. We climbed into the cozy glass-enclosed shower stall together, letting the water cascade over our bodies, replacing the aroma of chocolate with the sweet scent of pricey hotel soap.

A half-hour later Millie and I sat holding hands in the first row of the mezzanine of the New Amsterdam Theater, watching Simba navigate the tricky path of manhood in *The Lion King*. As the elaborately staged show unfolded at the Times Square showplace, I kept pulling Millie's mind back to our suite, whispering, "Can't wait to get you back in the room," or words to that effect. Millie loved it when I talked dirty, and I was determined to be the man she wanted me to be. I didn't want to just be the dutiful boyfriend. I wanted the weekend to be a passionate manifestation of my commitment to her because, in the one and a half years we'd been seeing each other, Millie often complained that our relationship was not the focus of my life.

We'd met at a jazz concert by the Lincoln Center Orchestra in Central Park. As Wynton Marsalis blasted through a solo, an investment banking couple introduced me to this nice black girl from the West who happened to be involved in lending money to cutting-edge Internet technology companies. Daughter of a schoolteacher and a nurse, married at twenty-three, divorced at twenty-six, dedicated to achievement, accomplishment and the pursuit of "fun stability," a curious phrase that meant a lot to Millie.

She'd passed up many a Wall Street buppie because they were too stable and not fun enough. She'd let go of a couple of music biz types who were fun but far too unstable. Somehow I'd managed, in her eyes, to be both fun and stable. I'm not quite sure how I'd done it but, this special weekend, I planned to reward her gernerous vision.

Our relationship had evolved organically. Three months in I cut off my other women. Six months in I let her answer my phone. Nine months in we spent two weeks island-hopping in the Caribbean. After a year I allowed her, finally, to put her voice on my answering machine tape. At every opportunity I praised Millie's cooking, her taste in clothes, even the way she handled her customers. I never complained when she left bed at three in the morning to check e-mail, and I worked hard not to let my eyes glaze over when the conversation turned to "domain names," "URLs" and "hits." Whenever my interest in her dot-com conversations wavered, I'd just stare into her bright, black eyes and glance down at those succulent gams, and I was cool.

After the final curtain we sauntered over to Jezebel's on Forty-fifth Street and Ninth, where we dined Creole style and laughed our way through a bottle of Moët. Jezebel's, with its dark bronze lighting, antique fixtures and embroidered draperies, always reminds me of a New Orleans bordello or, at least, my clichéd vision of one. Millie loved Jezebel's because it made her feel "like I'm not in New York but someplace different, someplace special." I couldn't argue with that—I felt the same. In the cab back to the Rhiga I rubbed those magnificent legs while she rested her head on my shoulder.

That, I'm happy to report, was the calm before a long, loud storm. With our bellies full and our desires whetted by the chocolate appetizer, we went right to the main course. Making love to Millie required patience and stamina. She never peaked quickly. I mean, if homegirl even moaned loud in the first fifteen minutes, I knew she was faking.

You see, Millie had a hooded clit. Things like the Godiva tongue bath were necessary to get her going because her clit, though sweet, needed substantial cultivation. So instead of one steady rhythm, I'd learned to stroke Millie with hesitating moves that broke up the beat and added drama to the proceedings. Meanwhile she would move her legs and shift her lower body to create opportunities for that clit to be rocked at different angles.

Once I found a rhythm she liked, Millie twisted herself around my head guiding me to just the right spot, then I'd go deep and stay regular as a heartbeat. Millie would then roll her pelvic muscles and control the horizontal herself. A lot of women let a small clit minimize the pleasure of sex, but Millie was smart and aggressive enough to understand the dos and don'ts of her fine brown frame.

We started in the middle of the bed but ended up half on, half off, with her head dangling over the edge and my head over hers, my sweat dripping onto her neck. I looked down at her—her mouth open, her eyes closed—and suddenly we were on the ledge of a skyscraper. The city of New York was spread out before me—the cars, the people, the buildings—a backdrop for Millie's ecstatic face. Millie was a Goddess, a glowing beautiful vision of rapture hovering over the metropolis. I tripped on this for a moment before I grunted like a grave digger and finally came.

When I woke up I felt dizzy. Rays of Manhattan sunlight slithered around the curtain's edge. Clothes, the remote and used condoms were scattered around the bedroom as in an abstract painting. The double doors were closed, but I could hear the familiar light taps and pings that told me Millie was on-line.

I rolled over and worked to suppress my anger. It was nine A.M. during a romantic weekend when people should, in my humble opinion, either be sleeping, eating or fucking (and not in that order either). So, why was she working? A year ago I would have caused an argument just by asking that question. And Millie would have answered, "Just because you're asleep, it doesn't mean everyone else is," or words to that effect.

No need to revisit that beef. Not now. Not this moment. Instead I went into the bathroom and stood patiently waiting for my pee to push its way past the backed-up sperm and exit. This was my least favorite part of sex—that morning-after piss.

It was as if your dick had to suddenly shift gears, going from pleasure center to waste-disposal unit.

When I opened the double doors, Millie was at the desk by the window wearing only her metal-rimmed Oliver Peoples glasses and the black La Perla camisole and panties I'd bought her last summer. Her fingers raced across the keyboard like a squirrel in spring. Breakfast was spread out on the coffee table. Eggs, croissants, fresh fruit, orange juice and herbal tea. It was a cute scene but it reminded me too much of being at her apartment on any old weekend. "Hey," I announced, "this looks too normal."

"Yeah? Well," she said, not looking up from the screen, "what do you suggest?"

When I said, "Let's do yoga," Millie replied with a big sunshine smile. And a few minutes later the computer sat alone, the table filled with breakfast had been pushed back and we were curled up like two pretzels on the hotel floor. In her eternal pursuit of flexibility and health, Millie had become a yoga aficionado over the past six months. She'd been studying at some spot on the West Side and been cajoling me to get busy with her. So far I'd resisted, though I often found it sexy watching her assume twisty positions with her legs and torso stretching before me on Saturday mornings.

Still, for me, a nonwork morning should mean a long, leisurely sleep, augmented by tossing, turning and some eye-rolling sex before breakfast. This yoga thing had become a weekend-morning cock blocker.

But this Saturday was going to be different. Instead of complaining, I dutifully followed along as Millie showed me the postures of the Sun Salutation. In fact, I found a couple of yoga poses I actually liked—standing on my left leg, my right one braced inside my thigh, with my right arms twisted before me like a strawberry Twizzler. I was surprised that I could pull off the balance this "tree" posture required. Millie was always telling me that my body type—six foot, lean and lanky—made me an excellent yoga specimen. I was beginning to believe her when she crawled over to me and began tickling my dangling testicles with her tongue.

"Hey Mill, don't do that."

I started teetering backward but Millie just chuckled and used her hands to steady me. Now she went for the gusto, taking me in her mouth while her hands kept me upright. It was an awkward, fun feeling—standing on one foot getting head. Part of my brain was still balancing my body; another part was enjoying Millie's mouth. Finally my poor brain could no longer handle this pleasure and pain and, like a chopped tree, I tumbled over.

We both laughed, then started kissing and it was on again. Millie, despite our consistently negative HIV test results, had a staunch no condom/no nookie rule that I respected. Still that didn't prevent a spirited bout of sixty-nine. Millie's lips were full but her mouth was small, a wonderful combination for oral sex. Using her right hand as a guide, Millie rolled her tongue in small circles as my body shook with pleasure. There's this spot just below my head that, when flicked just right, makes my mouth open, my eyes water and sends deep, subterranean spasms of pleasure up my back. Well, Millie hit it one-two-three times and my six stopped nineing. I just flopped around like a beached whale, erupted volcano-like and then, like a dream deferred, dried up.

The rest of the day passed in a state of suspended animation. Breakfast was eaten slowly. Our shower was leisurely. Even putting on our clothes took hours. We strolled hand in hand through Central Park, watching kids and animals at the zoo, ran our toes through the Great Lawn's new spring grass and waited in line for tickets to Shakespeare in the Park. Morgan Freeman was King Lear, with Jada Pinkett as one of his infamous daughters, a brilliant casting call I was dying to see in action.

Since the theater is at Seventy-ninth Street on the park's west side, Millie was tempted to run over to her apartment on Columbus after we'd copped the tickets. But I insisted "If we were going to play tourist, we should play it all the way." We killed time watching softball games and eating too many cherry ices. Under a hazy yet soft Manhattan sky Millie and I watched Morgan Freeman wrestle the Bard into submission with his smooth enunciation and a deep, anguished delivery. Not many women I've dated would have submitted to Shakespeare on a romantic weekend, but Millie wasn't like many women I've dated—she was smarter, warmer and more loving. Sitting next to her under Central Park's inky blue sky, I realized, for the twentieth or thirtieth time since we'd met, how lucky I was.

After the play we strolled down Central Park West past all the other New Yorkers who hadn't escaped the rock on this beautiful weekend. We saw homeless men and wayward children. We saw large families headed home from picnics and teens headed to parties and clubs. And we saw other lovers who held each other tighter than an accountant does a ledger.

At the corner of Central Park West and Sixty-third Street we spotted two black women — one five-foot-three with short, slick hair, the other five-eight or so with curly hair streaked blond — kissing so intensely I thought they'd suffocate. The shorter woman was twisting and turning her head so no corner of her lover's mouth would be unexplored. The taller woman used her long fingers to cradle her lover's fat, round bottom. She had dark brown fingers and a shining gold band on her index finger.

"Stop staring."

"Am I staring, Millie?" I replied with a guilty grin.

"Yes. And in the wrong direction."

I nuzzled Millie's neck with my nose and whispered, "Do I kiss you like that, Millie?"

"I can't remember," she said with a smirk. "Let's go back to the room and see."

We were supposed to go dancing at NV downtown. Or see Roy Hargrove at the Iridium. Those plans all got scrapped once we'd slipped off our shoes and started knocking boots all over the suite. In the shower. By the window. Millie rode me and I took her lying on our sides. We kissed so much I no longer could distinguish the taste of my mouth from the flavor in hers.

On Sunday we did nothing but sleep, order room service and rub our sore muscles with body oil. She tapped on her computer a bit. I reluctantly pulled out some clippings on next week's guests. That night I washed her hair as my mind slipped into work mode. Then, after we'd packed up our clothes and practiced some decidedly nonsexual yoga, Millie sat on the bed, looked at me balefully and started to cry.

"What's the matter, baby?" I reached out to touch her and she recoiled. "What's up?"

Instead of answering, Millie got up and went into the bathroom, locking the door behind her. This could have been the beginning of a shouting match with much banging on the door. I could have sat by the door pleading for Millie to come out and talk to me. I did neither. She had to come out eventually; I had nowhere to go. So I just sat on the bed and watched *SportsCenter*, one eye on the tube, the other on the bathroom door.

After a half-hour or so my lover emerged with eyes as red and watery as cheap wine.

"I thought you were going to propose to me," she said, suppressing a sob. My woman was crying—crying accusing tears. "If we were just gonna screw all weekend, we could have done that in Cancun."

"But," I said, before the whole relationship dissolved because I was slow and scared, "we aren't in Cancun and we're not together here just to get down." I went over to my travel bag, pushed aside my copy of the Knicks schedule and audience research, and pulled out the blue Tiffany's box I'd been waiting for just the right moment to produce since Friday night.

"Oh," she said as I opened it.

There had been at least three or four prime moments for me to reveal the box this weekend, yet a part of me held back each time, getting some perverse enjoyment out of the knowledge that I could change her mood forever by simply displaying it.

As I slipped the ring on her finger, I said apologetically, "I'm sorry it got to the point that you felt like crying, Mill. I guess there was a rhythm to this weekend—you felt it, you felt what I was supposed to do, but I'd procrastinated past the right moment. I hope the fact that I was a little slow in giving this to you doesn't mean you'll say no."

She silently looked down at the ring as I continued: "I believe this ring belongs to my future wife. And, you know, I believe you are that woman. I do love you, Mildred Jackson. I just need to know: Will you marry me?"

Millie's tear ducts swelled. Her womanly voice got squeaky. Her bright cheeks could have lit up Forty-second Street. I believe she said "I will," but I couldn't really hear 'cause her arms, her shoulders, her entire body engulfed me. I was covered now, not just by my woman's body, but by her spirit too. I was in a new place; some space I'd never visited before. I was happy. I was also very afraid.

Chapter 2

———— ⁊ ————

Maybe global warming is for real. I mean, I'm not qualified to prove or disprove that idea, but something's definitely up. This morning the weather shifted from fine spring seventies to midsummer humidity, and I found myself imagining Millie and me on a Central Park bench making out in the hot sun. Turning my attention back to business, I was back in our peach-colored conference room sitting in front of a framed poster of Nick Shaw, my boss and the host of our show. Around me at a table capable of seating twelve were my coworkers—the director, executive producer, art director, production coordinators and other functionaries.

To my immediate right: my assistant, Tanya Boston, a pink-lipped, thick-black-haired biracial graduate of Syracuse University who had been with me for three years and had developed into such a research demon that I was always fending off other shows vying for her services. She was quite cute, but I never messed with her, which I saw as a testament to my love for Millie.

At my left: Nick Shaw, our square-jawed, sandy-haired host, a television journalist turned heartthrob for overweight housewives and a few obsessed gay men. He had got me hired. For that I owed Shaw my loyalty. Yet there was something about owing my gig to this white man that irked me.

I wasn't just there as the token Negro. I was the segment producer who prepared Nick for all his interviews and I had a major hand in selecting the guests. Since this was primarily an interview show with some taped location bits, I had a pretty big gig. Few black people had this much input into a nationally syndicated nonwhite show. But not many people knew about me. I kept out of *Essence, Jet, Black Enterprise,* etc. I preferred to live the down-low life.

We were gathered together this morning for our biweekly demographic update, when a representative of the syndicator came in to tell us who was watching, why they watched, and what these numbers meant. I was always wary of these gatherings since my decisions as segment producer always seemed in question. Shaw tended to listen to me, which was flattering, but whenever there was "concern" about the show's direction, he and everyone else made me the whipping boy. Shaw often told people, "Dean is the conscience of the show." Sometimes I got the feeling this was more a complaint than a compliment.

In front of the conference room, Walker, a very stout, remarkably pale man, whose first name I never remembered, stood next to a video screen filled with numbers. "Our females in every age group are solid," Walker intoned monotonously. "Our eighteen to thirty-fours. Our thirty-fours and up. Even our males thirty-four and up are very competitive."

Walker's voice showed a hint of enthusiasm at that last point and I tried not to laugh as Nick nudged me in the ribs.

Then, pointing at a row of low numbers, Walker said, "But our eighteen to thirty-four male numbers are low to the point of invisibility."

"And I know why." It was Nick, talking in that brisk, crisp tone that made your ears snap to attention on camera and off.

"Well, Mr. Shaw, we have plenty of research on this subject."

"I'm sure you do, Walker, but the issue is as simple as night versus day. Men don't wanna fuck me."

"Well, uh," Walker stammered, "that's to be expected."

"That's right," Nick said. "We agree on that too." Nick hopped out of his seat and strode to the front of the room. I found myself sinking down into my seat. Nick's smirk meant trouble. So to pop his bubble a bit I announced, "Ladies and gentlemen, *The Nick Shaw Show*."

Ignoring me, Nick said smoothly, "What we need to do is give guys something to look at, something to lust for, something to tell their boys about when they're taking a break from discussing the Rock, Mankind and the rest."

Walker, desperate to resume control of the meeting, offered: "Our research shows you need more women in the eighteen to twenty-five demographic as guests."

Nick rapped on the video screen and then turned toward me. "T&A. Or, if you'll excuse the expression, tits and ass. That's what those numbers mean. But my segment producer, my main man, the conscience of my show, always has me talking to important people about important things, so that I have to do heavy lifting all the damn time."

To which I told my boss, "Which we do 'cause you're good at it, Mr. Emmy Winner. You like working your mental biceps."

"Yessss," he said, stretching it out and setting me up for a mocking comeback. He turned toward Walker. "But we need young male viewers, right, Walker?"

"Yes," he answered, resigned to his second-banana role. "It would help increase our ad rates."

"Hear that, Dean? To me that sends a clear message. It says to me we need a sprinkling of bimbos, more music and maybe a hint of violence. Right, Walker?"

"Sounds right," Walker replied quickly.

"Sounds like something my top staff people should be focusing on. Right, Dean?"

"Sounds right, boss," I said grudgingly.

"Well, then it sounds like we're finished. Staff lunch is on Walker here and his research department. Right, Walker?"

An unhappy Walker parted his lips to say, "Sounds right," as our staff began picking up papers, coffee cups and Palm Pilots. Shaw came over to me and laid his hands on my shoulders. "Just think T&A until sweeps are over. We've made a niche. Now let's go for the gold, Dean. We'll bring Pat Buchanan and Jesse Jackson back later. Okay, buddy?"

"It's your show."

"Only," he said with his TV smile, "when it's working."

I walked back to my office, headed toward what was the most important tool for processing information in talk television—a wall of index cards stuck on corkboard. We had computers, DVDs, and more VCRs than Sears, yet all the producers, the bookers, the network executives, the syndicators and even our genial host still had multicolored index cards pinned to the corkboard hung on their office walls. I walked up to mine and surveyed it.

The yellow cards represented booked guests and pretaped segments. The light blue cards represented offers that were out. Pink was for a segment or an idea in development. The red was for a guest or segment that was on someone's personal wish list. I spent a lot of my time at my board, tacking up cards, removing cards and gazing at the board, trying to get an idea of how the show was flowing, where there were holes and wondering how I could fill them.

Also on my corkboard wall were the names of regulars we had on two or three times a year—Al Sharpton, Bob Bennett, Stanley Crouch, Alan Dershowitz, Henry Louis Gates, Toni Morrison, Jane Pratt, Jane Alexander, Jimmy Carter—a worthy collection of pols, public figures, writers, editors and opinion givers who had enough attitude, juice and personality to keep Nick Shaw on his toes.

Then there were topics that we did repeatedly: teen suicide, teen murder, teen drug use; hip-hop as commodity, culture and curse; crimes against, by and for whites and blacks; making, losing and finding money; the Internet, pro and con; government corruption, incompetence and waste; big business exploitation, growth and dividends.

Those were the building blocks of our daily show. We did the odd piece on international affairs. The environment popped up whenever disaster struck. We rarely hit race head-on. Instead we rolled it into more general subjects, exploring how it played itself out in a variety of areas. This was my idea. As the only African-American executive on the show, I preferred not to do "RACISM!" but to see it as a part of general problems. That way my black talking heads got to vent on "general topics" and we rarely had shows where black and white (and Hispanic) folks spent the whole show hollering at each other.

It was also, I must admit, my idea that relationships were low on the totem pole of topics. Sex, romance, love, marriage, divorce, etc., were the stuff of every damn thing on the tube— you name the format and it exploits one of these subjects. So I'd helped make *The Nick Shaw Show* a space where other issues, other obsessions could be discussed and, when possible, exploited for our ratings gain. We never wallowed in the mud—we just got a little muck on our boots now and then. Or, I should say, we used to.

TO: MJACKSON@CKFS.COM

FROM: DCHANCE@SHAWSHOW.COM

SUBJECT: SEX

HEY MILL,

Strange news. The syndicator wants us to increase our young male numbers. Shaw suggested the way to do it was to add T&A to our guest rosters. So now Tanya and I have been seeking out strippers, pimps and sex salespeople of every description. Considering your performance last weekend, I'm thinking of booking you.

So how are things in mall America? Where are you today? Phoenix? San Antonio? Inquiring minds wanna know where their heart is.

TO: DCHANCE@SHAWSHOW.COM

FROM: MJACKSON@CKFS.COM

SUBJECT: RE: SEX

DEE,

I'm in Portland tonight and head down to the Bay Area tomorrow. Things are going well. The investments we've made out here are looking very smart. We've found a few things that looked better on-line than in the flesh but, for the most part, no bad surprises.

Just to get you jealous, a few of my clients look better in person than through my DSL line. I'm using my engagement ring as kryptonite to weaken all would-be Supermen. But I must say, I think you got to me just in time, slowpoke.

As for the show, I think there are ways to talk about sex intelligently on broadcast TV. If anyone can make it happen, you can, Dean. Just pull out that wonderful inner freak you save for special occasions.

I think it's interesting that Nick Shaw suggested this direction. There's a whole lot of kink in that all-American boy.

Love from your future wife.

Chapter 3

Mid-afternoon a few days later and I'm at my desk looking out at an overcast Manhattan sky. The upper floors of the midtown skyscrapers out my window were obscured by thick, gray clouds.

"I have the Reverend Arthur Brown on the line for you, Mr. Chance" a very officious, black church lady's voice told me. My computer clock read 2:15 P.M.

"But I thought the Reverend wouldn't be available until three."

"His schedule has changed and he's available now. He's very anxious to speak to you."

"Okay," I said, and then began pulling out my notes, clicking my screen to the page with my questions and flipping on the speakerphone. "Please, put him on."

"Hold on a minute, Mr. Chance," the voice said.

There was a pause, a bit of cell phone static and then I was put on hold.

"Tanya!" I shouted. "Tanya!"

"Yes, Dean." My assistant appeared at my door with a mouth full of lettuce.

"Hold my calls and close the door. I have Reverend Art on the line."

"Dean, they told me they wouldn't call until three."

"You know how this works, Tanya. The Reverend has my private line and you know his mantra, 'I work on the people's schedule.'"

"Mr. Chance?" that officious female voice inquired from the speakerphone.

"Right here."

"The Reverend has been momentarily detained. We'll call right back." I gave a polite "No problem" and clicked off the speaker.

Ah, the pre-interviews. The backbone of my job—the reason I get paid, the key to my success. And an absolute pain in my ass. During the pre-interview I talk to the guest in order to choreograph the "spontaneous" conversation millions will see. It's often tricky making this happen when you have high-profile guests busy doing high-profile things, but it's essential if a guest's appearance is going to run smoothly and have maximum impact.

On the late-night shows like Leno and Letterman the pre-interview is the Bible. The topics, anecdotes, funny stories and gags agreed upon become the template for every word spoken on camera. Basically that chat is as scripted as a sitcom and often just as rote.

On the rawer, exploitative shows like Springer, Lake, etc., where the unexpected revelation, those "gotcha" moments, are the core of the broadcast, the pre-interviews are designed to identify embarrassing material and figure out how to instigate outrage. Like the explosions in a big action movie, those shows live for the explosive "oooohs!" generated by angry wives, girlfriends and the ever-popular baby mothers.

The morning shows are a mix of choreography and improvisation. If the guest is hyping an album, movie or TV show, the interview is basically composed of predictable questions about whatever they're hawking, though Bryant Gumble or Katie Couric are capable of blindsiding a guest with a provocative personal question. The difference between them and Jenny Jones is that the question is asked, not with an exploitative sneer, but with the false gravity of the "serious" reporter.

Now, on nontabloid, nonexploitative programs, if the guest is involved in a breaking news story or is a prominent politician/public figure, a category that includes mayors, senators, congresspeople, social activists, widows of crime victims, journalists, authors and criminals, there is a pre-interview but a slender script. The interviewer often actually interviews the guest. Real follow-up questions and real unexpected queries. The possibility for anger and conflict. And the chance that the whole interview could fall flat since those three or four minutes of prime television time rely on the energy—either sympathetic or combative—between the people on screen.

On *The Nick Shaw Show* we sought a balance between tightly arranged talk and totally improvised debate. Which is why I wanted to talk with the controversial, though increasingly mainstream, politician, and also why it was no surprise that Reverend Art was proving elusive. I'd waited hours for stars and politicians to meet for our appointed chat. And, basically, I had to take it. It's my job to talk with them, to make myself available per their schedule, even if they (and their staff) treat me as disrespectfully as a marine drill instructor does his recruits.

Today I'd scheduled two important pre-interviews—one with the aforementioned Reverend Art and the other with Missy DeMann, a dominatrix with a clientele reputedly packed with Wall Street suits, high-court judges and a well-known TV celebrity or two. Even better for us, Miss DeMann only serviced white men. It seemed this African-American dominatrix was a whipping, spanking embodiment of Jim Crow. Tanya had unearthed this lady, which made me put a big gold star next to her name.

She and I began our talk this morning, but a client paged her for some emergency discipline from this lady's paddle. "I'll get back at ya, honey," Missy DeMann told me saucily. "I just have to go 'head and wave my magic wand."

So I was also waiting on her. Since the sepia dominatrix was part of the *Shaw Show*'s New World Order, I needed to do the pre-interview. Brown was a regular, and so I should have been able to let Tanya handle that pre-interview. But Shaw would have flipped if anybody but me spoke with Reverend Art or any of the bigger names.

So on days like this I just get comfortable, light the Aveda calming candles Millie gave me and chill out. I ordered a tuna on whole wheat, an apple juice and some grapes—provisions for my usual afternoon of cell phone static, note taking and "That's very interesting" murmured by me like I really cared.

The dominatrix called back first. "Well, it's like this, Dean

Chance," she said with the vigor of a woman used to a man's undivided attention. "There are no people on earth who need a good spanking more than men who make decisions. They are masters of their universe, and that kind of pressure needs an outlet."

"Why not some yoga, a good massage and some steam?"

DeMann answered, "Not quite painful enough, Dean Chance. My sessions are like exorcism. I purify them of the guilt that comes from moving people around like chess pieces. I let them be the victim. In my dungeon they can be weak and it has no consequences. Their psychological barriers fall, so that when they go back to work, they have a mind clear of bad conscience and all the mental clutter that accompanies it."

"Okay, so why only white men? Black men don't need a bit of stress relief?"

"Dean Chance, are you black?"

"Yes, I am."

"Well, this next answer is off the record. Alright, brother Dean Chance?"

"Okay. What's the real deal?"

"Well, I have several *very* prominent black clients. But I've found that my public policy is a turn-on for both white and black men."

"And how's that work?"

"Well, Dean Chance, the white men feel like they have an exclusive, discriminating woman beating, peeing and ordering them about."

"And the brothers feel they're getting something extra special, something the white men don't know about. It makes it sweeter. Am I on the right track?"

"Dean Chance," she said, sounding intrigued, "you seem to understand all this very well."

I got a buzz on the intercom from Tanya and put Missy DeMann on hold.

"It's Reverend Art, Dean."

"Okay, give me thirty seconds."

Back to Missy DeMann. "I'm sorry but I have to cut this short for now. I have another guest I have to talk with."

"And Dean Chance, who would you leave Missy DeMann for? I'm nosy."

"Missy DeMann, I would only bump you for someone extra special. I have Reverend Arthur Brown on the line and he's a hard man to get."

"Don't I know it," she said seriously. "My nephew got arrested unfairly by the police, so I set up a meeting with the Reverend. Met with him one time, but after that, it was hard getting a follow-up meeting. I guess it's hard being a man who makes things happen."

"Sounds like a potential client."

"Wouldn't you like to know, Dean Chance?" she teased. "If you have any other questions, I have no other appointments this afternoon. If you wanna stop in, let me know. Bye."

That was a weird way to end that conversation. Did Missy DeMann sense something in me? She made me a bit uncomfortable, but this wasn't the time to dwell on that. I just shook it off and switched gears for Reverend Art. The topic was the Democratic Party's relationship to black voters so far in the twenty-first century. A typical *Nick Shaw Show* subject and the good Reverend, longtime sound-bite master, was a pro and the pre-interview went by quickly.

But Missy DeMann's playful comment lingered in my mind. So before signing off, I mentioned casually how strange a day it had been. "I mean," I said, "it's quite a contrast speaking to you now, Reverend Art, after who I'd spoken to earlier." I was hoping, despite the many topics on Reverend Art's mind, including voter registration and the liberation of brown peoples worldwide, that his curiosity might be piqued.

He bit. "Who did you talk to, Dean? Giuliani? Pataki?"

"No, a black dominatrix."

"A dominatrix? Really." The Reverend chuckled. "Was this for your pleasure or is she to be a guest?"

"A guest, Reverend. We're trying to find ways to deal with sex but in a serious, nonexploitative manner."

"Interesting."

"Indeed. We found this black woman who in fact discriminates in her domination. Only has white clients. At least that's what she tells people. Sounds like maybe you should lead a protest march outside her condo."

"What's this young lady's name?"

"Missy DeMann. You want the number, Reverend?"

"No, Dean," he said, laughing louder than before. Then half-joking, half-serious, he said, "You should be careful booking people like that. It could hurt your credibility. What will my constituents think of me sharing a stage with someone like that?"

"Honestly, Reverend, I worry about that too. But we've made the commitment and we're gonna see how it works out.

But when you come in, you should mention this to Nick Shaw."

"I definitely will, Dean. See you in a few days."

After he'd hung up I got a bit depressed. We'd worked so hard to develop the show into something meaningful. Now this sex stuff could alienate our quality guests. Once one or two prominent people turned us down, it could have a nasty ripple effect.

I was mulling this over and picking at my grapes when the other paddle dropped.

"Dean," Tanya said via the intercom, "I have Missy DeMann on the line. Says it's urgent."

"Missy DeMann," I said happily. "Ready to resume?"

"I'm sorry, Dean Chance, but I called to tell you I'm not doing your show."

"Oh," I said, shocked. "What is it? Is there anything I can do? We could disguise your face or voice?"

"No, Dean Chance. It's just that my spiritual advisor feels I need to maintain a low profile, and when God's messenger calls, little black girl's gotta listen."

"Your spiritual advisor?"

"That's right. Even dominatrices go to church, Dean Chance."

My imagination, which can take some wild turns, filled with the image of Missy DeMann in a pink-veiled hat and white stockings exiting Reverend Art's uptown cathedral, followed closely by a second image, that of the Reverend in a dog collar barking at Missy DeMann's unforgiving orders.

"Okay. It's certainly your decision. You were doing us a real favor appearing on the show. Tell you what—I'm gonna send you some tickets to the show. Come in, watch a taping. Maybe you'll change your mind."

"What a nice offer, Dean Chance. I'll come by sometime."

"One more question, Missy DeMann: Why do you use both my first and last name when you address me?"

"Dean Chance, I've found that there's something about saying both names that makes most people uncomfortable. It reminds them of being scolded by their mother and father, or being called out by their teacher or school principal. First and last names said repeatedly are the sounds of discipline to most people and, as you know, discipline is my business."

"Okay, thanks for the explanation. Now would you please reconsider your decision?"

"Probably not, Dean Chance. But if you ever feel like letting go, cleansing yourself of your need to control things, just dial me up. I'm sure I can squeeze you in."

"Thanks again for the offer, but I got engaged just this past weekend, so I've found a woman that fulfills that particular part of my life."

"If you say so, Dean Chance," she said, sounding unconvinced. "If you say so."

Show & Tell

<YOU HAVE RECEIVED AN INVITATION FROM SEECEE TO JOIN A PRIVATE CHAT ROOM>

<ALADY27 ENTERS THE ROOM>

SeeCee: Glad to have you with us, Alady27, but I'm not particularly happy with the fact that you haven't joined the conversation. It's been four weeks. You know lurking is against my rules.

Alady27: I know that you like participation. But I've always been more interested in watching and listening than being active myself. I'm hearing things in your chat room that I've never come across. I've always been intrigued by the idea of watching sex. Not pornography, but those stolen moments between people. Kissing passionately in the park. A hand under a dress at a fancy restaurant. Peering into a bedroom whose window is just a little too open. That's what interests me, SeeCee.

SeeCee: Well, well. Now that I know what you're looking for, I can be very helpful. Why don't we continue this dialogue over e-mail? I have some images I think you'll enjoy.

Chapter 4

It's Friday of our first week attempting to add sex to our interviews and things have been very frustrating. Either we were looking in the wrong places or people thought Tanya and I were vice cops, not television producers seeking vice. After losing Missy DeMann and getting the cold shoulder from others, I'd decided to hire a consultant with contacts in the sex world to act as a guide to the best available sleaze. When I came in this morning, Tanya felt she'd found our sexual surrogate.

"Okay, you say that this Professor Lawson is good?"

"Absolutely." Tanya sat across the desk from me, anxious as a bookworm aching to be Homecoming Queen. "He teaches classes at NYU on both sexuality and pop culture. He's written three books—the last one, *Sexual Seeing*, got him a rave review in the *Times* and is used in many schools around the country. He contributes to Nerve.com and lectures all over. He's been married three times. He's forty-three and advocates couples joining swing clubs to save their marriages. And he's black. I think he'd be an excellent resource."

"Okay," I said. "Did you tell him this was just a get-to-know-you call?"

"Absolutely. He knows nothing's definite."

"Okay," I said, and then dialed his number. "Sorry I'm being so stern, but after that mess with the Reverend and the dominatrix, I just wanna keep everything under control."

"Absolutely," Tanya replied.

A deep, manly, Barry White-esque "hello" flowed through my speakerphone.

"Hello, Professor, this is Dean Chance and Tanya Boston of *The Nick Shaw Show*."

"Hi, Professor," Tanya cooed.

"Hello, Tanya," he answered suavely. "You're very prompt, Mr. Chance. A nice quality. One doesn't like to wait too long for pleasure."

"Pleasure? I've never thought of a professional interview as 'pleasure,' Professor. Dental work is how it sometimes feels on my end."

"I can only imagine. Tanya tells me you're a very hard worker."

"Thank you, Tanya," I said, smiling, "but no more than the next man. Tanya has shown me some of your work. Pretty provocative."

"Thanks. I'm flattered." Then he went into a slick prepackaged rap: "I believe I can help you move your show into the world of tasteful eroticism. Most TV producers see erotic topics as either a danger to the country or a joke—a jerk, an orgasm and a Handi Wipes."

"Isn't that all there is to it?" I said, joking.

"Well, for some people, mostly men, it is. But there's more going on than that. Sex penetrates every level of our conscious and unconscious mind. For your show to acknowledge that, and to do it tastefully, will help puritanical Americans see that. And it won't be bad for your ratings either."

"No question," I said.

"I see it," the Professor continued, "as something of a mission to open up the topic of sexuality in this country—one narrow mind at a time. AIDS has frightened people away from the true pleasures that can be had by consenting, mature adults in controlled yet passionate situations."

"Well, Professor, the management of this show wanna open up minds as well and it's my job to make that happen. Yet I do wonder whether, between music videos, Victoria's Secret and the whole world of Web sex, our culture is not already drowning in a sea of undulating breasts and male backsides."

I could hear the Professor take a deep breath. Sounded like I'd pissed him off, yet his reply was measured. "It's all about context, Dean. The difference between exploitation and understanding is context."

"Okay," I said with a slight edge of cynicism in my voice. "Tanya has told me that you're an aggressive advocate of swinging, which I assume means you share your wife with other men?"

"That's correct."

"So what's the context for that, Professor? Is watching your wife have intercourse with other men while you have intercourse with their wives really a way to celebrate love and build trust?" Realizing I was probably sounding as judgmental as a Catholic priest, I added, "I'm just playing devil's advocate here, Professor."

"Of course," he said smugly. "Just trying to understand

what you clearly don't." My face must have flushed because Tanya cut in, saying, "Tell him about *The Ethical Slut*, Professor."

"Of course, Tanya. *The Ethical Slut* is a book many people who are serious about loving their mate and having sex with others view as a kind of Bible. The emphasis in the book is not on the slut, but on how to ethically, respectfully and with total candor allow yourself and your mate to express sexual desire while maintaining strong bonds of fidelity and commitment. I've never engaged in swing behavior without making people aware of the philosophy behind the acts. I believe true sexual expression is only possible in an atmosphere of honesty and openness."

"There are no secrets between you and your wife?"

"I don't allow them."

"Come on, Professor, doesn't total honesty in a relationship lead to total chaos? It creates resentment. It creates anger. You know and I know that having a selective memory is a very useful tool."

"I know what you're getting at, Dean, but I can't agree. If you're open to experimentation, have a good time. If you're conservative, live up to those values. It's the person who denies his true nature that not only ends up frustrating his mate, but, in my experience, often ends up repressing others to mask their inner selves."

After his very passionate spiel I felt I'd been too flip, too dismissive, so I decided to add: "I really hope you take my comments in the context of getting to know your views, Professor. I really meant no offense."

"Not at all, Dean. My life is about this all day, all night."

For the next twenty minutes we talked specifically about the show: how he could be a liaison between the show and sex professionals; how he could direct us to articulate people in the industry, or alert us to legislation or government policies that would impact sexuality. The Professor was witty, intelligent and seemingly well connected, yet I was shocked at how edgy the discussion made me. It was as if our talk about AIDS, transsexuals, call girls and sex shops was opening some door in my psyche. What was in that adjoining room clearly scared me. Moreover, it was like the Professor could feel my discomfort through the speakerphone. I was wrapping up the discussion when the Professor inquired, "Dean, can I ask you a few questions?"

"More about the show?"

"No, about you. Sexually speaking. It'll help me help you if I have a better handle on where you're coming from."

"Okay," I replied, "but what do you mean 'coming from'?" I looked over at Tanya and she gave me an I-have-no-idea-what's-up look.

"You see, Dean, sex is such a subjective topic that, as I said earlier, in discussing it, a little context is always helpful. Tanya says you dress conservatively."

"I like a well-made suit as much as the next man."

"Is that what it is? Or perhaps you use your suits to hide the black man inside. A suit is a uniform that, under many circumstances, is used to sublimate a man's sexuality, to make the differences between him and other men disappear."

I actually thought this was a pretty interesting line of questioning—just not one I really wanted to get into. So I told him, "Professor, being black has nothing to do with how I dress or conduct myself at this office. I'm engaged to a very beautiful black woman. So at work and elsewhere I keep my well-pressed pants to myself." Then I laughed one of those share-the-joke-with-me laughs that I hoped would put an end to this conversation.

"I see, Dean. So no hanky-panky at the office?"

"Absolutely not. An office is for working—a playground or bedroom is for playing. I believe the two should be kept as separate as possible."

"I find the two inseparable," he replied. "And in my research I've found that offices are, in fact, a powerful site of sexual desire and fantasy, and that our clothes, even in a button-down environment, are full of signifiers. Your attention to detail may be significant."

"Are you psychoanalyzing me, Professor?"

"Oh no," he said with an unconvincing chuckle. "Just thinking out loud."

"Dean's just careful, Professor," Tanya interjected. "He's not a man who lets stuff get away from him."

"Thank you, Tanya."

"Just one more question then, Dean?"

"Go on. I hope this has been educational."

"You ever go on-line to a sexually oriented chat room?"

"No way. Not that I'd even know where to go. My fiancée's on-line all the time. I suppose," I said, smiling, "I should ask her, huh? But the truth is, good sex is harmony between the mind and the body, Professor. No computer allowed. Besides, I can't jerk off and type at the same time."

"I see," he said, amused. "Well, Dean, aside from learning I'm nosy, is there anything else you want to learn about me?"

I told the Professor "no," and than said real ass-kissy, "Thank you for your time and insights. It's really given us a lot to think about," before hanging up. I already knew what I needed to know—he could help the show and the guy obviously had balls. I mean, he'd tried to turn his job interview into a sexual interrogation of me. Plus he'd clearly been squeezing information out of Tanya and she, clearly enthralled with the guy, ended up talking way out of turn. A part of me wanted to turn him down, but at least initially we needed someone like him on the payroll. Once we'd done a few shows and had penetrated the sex biz, I'd ditch this inquisitive academic. So I told Tanya, "You deal with him from now on. Okay?"

"Absolutely."

"And under no circumstances do you promise him a spot on the air. He only gets consulting producer credit on the shows he helps us on. We're not making him a star unless we have to."

"Absolutely."

"And," I said with fatherly deliberation, "you are to get information from the Professor. You are not to tell him my or, for that matter, your business. This guy makes his living as an academic voyeur. You don't wanna end up in one of his text-books, do you?"

"Absolutely not," she replied with surprisingly little conviction.

"Secrets are good, Tanya. I treasure mine."

"Does Millie know you feel this way?"

"Of course not. That's why it's a secret."

Show & Tell

FROM: ALADY27@EARTHLINK.NET

TO: SEECEE@HOTMAIL.COM

SUBJECT: BUTTS

I downloaded the video you sent me. Fun to watch. I thought I'd be turned off but I actually enjoyed it. The sex was more intimate than I'd imagined. But I'm not likely to engage in that sort of behavior. My butt is sacred.

FROM: SEECEE@HOTMAIL.COM

TO: ALADY27@EARTHLINK.NET

SUBJECT: RE: BUTTS

Glad you enjoyed the footage. Glad you weren't shocked. Not so happy you don't actually wanna try liberating your lovely hind parts. I have lots and lots of videos. But I want something in return. Tell me about your love life. You like to watch; I like to hear. I'll show you mine; you tell me yours. Show & Tell. A bargain?

Chapter 5

———— ⤪ ————

stop in Barneys once a month. Not necessarily to buy anything but because I love to fondle a well-made suit. That may sound strange, and, if it does, so be it. I derive great pleasure from admiring pliant natural fabrics stitched together with an artist's eye and a craftsman's needle. In particular, I enjoy the soft, silky linings of a good suit, the kind that when you wear the right linen shirt rubs sweetly against your nipples. Encased snuggly in a well-lined suit, my body feels like it's being hugged through long days of meetings and ass kissing.

On this afternoon I'd sneaked out of the office and cabbed it over to the East Side to luxuriate in the uncomplicated pleasures of fondling fine fabric. I was on one knee in the Donna Karan section, touching the interior of a charcoal gray double-breasted number when a woman's voice asked me a strange question: "Which would you prefer?"

I turned and found two long, slender pieces of fabric dangling before me. On the right was a navy blue tie with small, subdued white diamonds arranged evenly across—a tie that would have made Newt Gingrich happy. Next to it was a Pucci tie spiced with bright, confrontational yellows and purples that would have brought joy to a Mediterranean gigolo. Presenting both ties carefully, like a doctor does a newborn to its mother, were long female fingers tipped with beautifully manicured nails. The ties were so close to my eyes that the questioner's face was a blur.

"Excuse me?"

"Which tie would you prefer? If you were buying."

The face slowly came into focus. Her skin was brown with a burnished red undertone. Her eyes were slender and vaguely Asian. She had a wide, full mouth and angular cheekbones that made her look both totally African and totally Native American, a blend that gave her face drama. Her legs had a sturdy I-love-the-Stairmaster shape visible through sheer black stockings. As I stood up I noticed the black skirt, gray sweater and black jacket that covered the rest of her lean, athletic body. Though she was dressed as a businesswoman, her body had the coiled energy of a sprinter just before the starter's gun.

"Well," I began, "that depends. What kind of man are you buying it for?" She smiled—a very weird one too—outwardly inviting, yet chilly as well.

"Someone," she said casually, "who looks like you."

"Okay," I said, trying to hide how unnerved I was by her insistent gaze. "If I were buying a tie today, I'd buy that one." I reached out and rubbed the blue tie between my thumb and forefinger.

"That's what I thought." She slid the blue tie from her fin-

gers while I smiled, expecting more conversation, some ban-
ter and a formal introduction. Instead she turned in her black
slip-ons and walked toward the counter.

A white salesman, who seemed quite pleased to serve her,
inquired, "You want both ties, miss?"

"No," she said firmly, "just this one."

She handed the salesman the more adventurous Pucci tie
and laid the blue one on the counter as if it were diseased.
When told the purchase would cost $110, she pulled out a
platinum American Express card and then cut me a sardonic,
amused look, as if she was enjoying some private joke with a
punch line that eluded me. I watched her for some gesture
that suggested I come over. Nothing. She just leaned down to
sign her bill. I mean, I shouldn't have cared. After all, I was
engaged. Still, I had an ego. I really would have enjoyed turning that lovely lady down.

"Mr. Chance." It was Gene, a cool gay salesman who often
helped me with my selections. "See anything you like today?"
I didn't answer immediately, so he followed my eyes to the
counter and smirked. "Afraid I can't help you with that purchase."

I said, "Yeah, well, looks like somebody already bought that
merchandise."

"You think so?" he replied doubtfully. "I don't know, Mr.
Chance. She looks like she owns herself."

Like a first-class sucker, I stood there watching this sexy
lady, awaiting a parting glance, a smile, a nod. Just some con-
tinuation of this little game. *Nada.* She turned and moved
away from me. Felt like it was July and I'd just missed the ice
cream truck. I hadn't started it. Guess it wasn't for me to finish.

"So," Gene started, "how's Millie these days?"

"Away, Gene," I replied. "Very far away."

Rain was falling as I exited onto Madison Avenue. A pewter shroud blocked out the sky. Spring rain usually makes me happy but I was still a little upset at being toyed with upstairs. Disgruntlement became irritation when a cab slowed down and then jetted past me to pick up a white woman half a block away. I was about to flag down another cab when a black sedan swerved in front of me, blocking the cab and damn near rolling over my foot.

Incensed, I walked over to the limo driver's window and slammed my palm against the sedan's hood. The driver, a burly brother with world-weary eyes, made an It's-not-me gesture with his hands and then aimed a thumb at his passenger. The sedan's tinted rear window rolled down and I, now even more irritated, stormed back to curse out the passenger.

Out of the dark backseat a woman's voice said: "Looks like you could use a lift." Instead of seeing a face, my eyes focused on a beautiful pair of bare feet. Coming out of the dark like a ship through fog was the face of the woman with the ties. It was one of those moments when a second is an hour and reality cracks like an egg. "Come on. Get in."

I was in the backseat before I knew it. We were gliding across Sixtieth Street before I felt myself sit down. It seemed like I should say something, so I mumbled, "Thanks. I appreciate it."

"My pleasure. Where to? Midtown, I'd imagine."

"Yeah. Good guess. Fifty-seventh Street and Tenth." I sat there awkwardly waiting for her to introduce herself. A few more seconds passed and she just chilled. So I stuck out my hand and told her, "My name's Dean Chance."

She caressed my hand when she touched it and said, "Bee Cole." Then she addressed the driver. "You're going to take Mr. Chance to Fifty-seventh and Tenth after you drop me off." He nodded quickly and hooked a left onto Fifth. It was her move and she made it decisively.

"Take your shoes off."

"Excuse me?"

That amused smile appeared and again she requested, "Take your shoes off." She raised up her beautiful shoeless feet and wiggled her toes. "I don't allow people to wear shoes in my house," she explained, "and this car is where I'm living now. So . . ."

Reluctantly I complied, slipping off my black loafers, an action that, under her gaze, made me feel absolutely naked. Bee smiled again. Her full lips and sharp white teeth both aroused and chilled me. Neither ashamed nor embarrassed, Bee boldly surveyed my feet. If I'd felt naked before, now I felt raped. It was eerie how the removal of my shoes and this woman's stare had so clouded my mind.

"So, Mr. Chance—"

"Dean," I said, trying again to gain some control.

"So, Dean, you married or divorced?"

I should have answered forthrightly, with no ducking or dodging. Instead I answered, "I'm seeing someone." If that wasn't weak enough, I volunteered, "We're almost married."

"Almost married?" She found that funny. "What did P-Funk say? That's like standing on the verge of getting it on. Is this condition a good or bad thing?"

I said forcefully—perhaps too earnestly—"We're engaged

and it's a very good thing." For a moment it got quiet. Then she started staring at my feet again. So I suggested, "Maybe I should put my shoes back on."

Looking up at my face, she wondered out loud, "Why?"

"The smell. My woman complains I sweat a lot."

"Nothing wrong with a man sweating," she replied. Then Bee admitted, "But I'm staring at your feet, aren't I?" She actually blushed and giggled. A good sign, I thought. A real human moment. Maybe Bee wasn't just a sexy psycho.

So I chuckled and agreed, "Well, yeah, you are."

I was beginning to relax when Bee flipped it again. "Don't mind me, Dean," she said matter-of-factly, "I just like looking at a man's extremities." I got that worried and aroused feeling again, but my new friend wasn't through. "I'm not looking for length, Dean. That feet-equals-length thing is for fools. It doesn't matter how long or small a man's feet are, it's the way they're put together that impresses me." She gave my feet the once-over again and then the car pulled up to the curve.

We were in the Fifties near Rockefeller Center. "I get off here," she announced. "Let me have your business card." I reached into my wallet and handed it to her. She looked at it and was, I believe, impressed. When I asked for hers, Bee grinned and told me, "I don't have any with me right now." Clearly she was lying, but that was cool. If she made a habit of picking up men in Barneys, I guess she had to be on the DL.

"Thanks for the ride, Bee," I said as she exited.

"Talk to you soon."

"Really?" I replied, hoping to squeeze a real answer out of her. Instead of another mysterious reply, Bee just reached back and kissed me on the cheek. The driver popped open an umbrella and escorted her to the lobby. From inside the car I watched her walk away from me and wondered if I'd ever see her again and, if I did, would that be a good thing.

FROM: SEECEE@HOTMAIL.COM

TO: ALADY27@EARTHLINK.NET

SUBJECT: RE: MY BIRTHDAY TREAT

Well, your man is certainly capable of exciting you. His efforts seem to be more than adequate. But if your man's imagination excites you, why do you need our show & tell?

I've attached the photos you requested about African sexual customs. They will be, I think, most instructive.

FROM: ALADY27@EARTHLINK.NET

TO: SEECEE@HOTMAIL.COM

SUBJECT: YOUR QUESTION

Why do I need our show & tell? Actually, until you brought it up, I didn't know the question was important. I know I love my fiancé and I know he is the future father of my children.

You, I enjoy. You've shown me things I'm happy to finally see and I'm so grateful for that. You're like a sexual toy for me. My fiancé couldn't be that.

As a token of our connection (and because you've requested it) I'm sending you a picture of me. It is not doctored. It is not taken from some magazine. It's me. When is yours coming my way?

Chapter 6

The next day at work a half dozen orchids arrived for me. My assistant, Tanya, brought them in. "Oh, this is sweet," she announced in that cooing way women have when they detect romance in the air. She carefully placed the orchids in a tall water glass, vowing to purchase a real vase at lunchtime.

"Isn't Millie sweet," Tanya gushed again as she handed me the card and then awaited its opening. I flipped open the eggshell-colored envelope and then my eyes grew wide as silver dollars.

"That must be some message." Tanya was anxiously trying to bend over to read it, but that wasn't a good idea. The orchids weren't from Millie. In red ink the card read, "For Your Pleasure." It was signed "Bee." I stuffed it in my shirt pocket.

"Too hot to share?" Tanya offered, still fishing tenaciously for facts.

"Yeah," I said and didn't lie when I added, "It was real intense."

Tanya screwed up her face at that, realizing that I wasn't giving up details. Changing the subject, I asked her to find out when the staff meeting was scheduled. As soon as she left the room I looked up Millie's hotel number in Phoenix and punched in the digits in a guilty flurry. It was 9:45 A.M. out West, making it likely Millie had been gone a couple of hours already.

Still, I wanted Millie to hear my voice as soon as she returned to her room. I wanted her to hear me proclaiming my love. I said I missed her and couldn't wait for her to return. I even offered to join her on the road. I urged her to call me back and not just send e-mail, since I was desperate to hear her voice. I tried to sound needy and lonely, but was afraid I'd only communicated confusion and guilt.

The next day another gift arrived. Actually two gifts in one box—the ties from Barneys. Like the orchids, they were hand-delivered and, like the orchids, they sparked another orgy of comments from Tanya: (a) "Millie is really romantic, isn't she?" (b) "You guys are really hot for each other, huh?" (c) "You think she'll stay this romantic after you're married?" and (d) "It's almost like you two just met, isn't it?"

Tanya's last comment stung, so I tried to make her seem immature. "This is just Millie's way of keeping the relation-ship fresh and exciting," I said quite matter-of-factly. But I could tell Tanya was getting suspicious. Refusing to let her peek at this second card didn't help. "The Ties That Bind," it said in red ink. This was not a sentence I wanted to explain to my assistant or to the other staff people Tanya would surely tell.

In a defensive maneuver, I had Tanya send Millie flowers in Denver, which, aside from being her hometown, was the next stop on her business sojourn.

What message was the mysterious Bee Cole sending me? That she wanted to "do" me seemed clear. And, just as obviously, there was more going on than simple lust. The gifts and the cards made me feel like a girl just off the bus from Minnesota being wooed by a Port Authority pimp. Men have run this game forever. The slick pickup line. The sexy rap. The gifts. The only thing missing was the follow-up phone call and the invitation to dinner.

That evening around six P.M. Tanya buzzed me. "It's a Bee Cole from Barneys. Is this about a present you're getting Millie?" I replied with a noncommittal "Maybe" and had the call put through.

"You sent me one tie too many."

"No. I don't think so."

"I told you I only liked the blue one."

"The blue tie is who you are now. The Pucci is for who you could become. Keep the other in the closet. It'll come out one day."

This is where I should have just blurted out, "I'm engaged! It was fun having you mack me, but never contact me again!" and hung up the phone. But of course I didn't. Instead: "When are we going to get together and have a real conversation?"

"Do you like basketball?"

"Had Knick season tickets since the year they drafted Patrick Ewing."

"Good. That makes it more fun."

"Does it, now?"

"Look for me at tonight's game."

"Well, what section are you in? The Garden's a big place."

"Keep your eyes open, Dean. If you're meant to find me, you will. If not, you still got two very nice ties out of the meeting. That should give you some satisfaction."

"You must think I'm easily satisfied."

"I don't know you well enough to say that, do I?" she replied. "But then time answers every question. See you at the Garden."

FROM: MJACKSON@CKFS.COM

TO: DCHANCE@SHAWSHOW.COM

SUBJECT: BUSY

Sorry I didn't get back to you sooner. I've been running, but the sweat I'm dripping is gonna help pay for our wedding. The travel has given me a lot of great ideas. Sometimes I think we should do it out West in a canyon. Sometimes I see us standing on a cliff above an ocean. I even have visions of the whole wedding party in old English outfits right out of *Shakespeare in Love.*

The other day in Austin I snuck into a wedding reception in the hotel ballroom and watched the bride throw the bouquet. It's amazing to think that'll be me real soon. I'm gonna be an MC aka Millie Chance. Can't wait.

I love you.

Chapter 7

———— ⸗ ————

Section 219. Madison Square Garden. Sixty-three bucks a pop.

"Why shouldn't she expect a ring?" This was David talking.

"Yeah," I replied.

"Absolutely," David continued. "It's to be expected. She's of that certain age. The biological clock tick, tick, ticks away. You're a good catch. You basically treat her nice. And it's been about two years—two years in the dating life of a woman over thirty is like five years in a man's life. The clock ticks. The eggs get cold. And a good man like you does the right thing."

"What a woman expects and what she gets don't have to be the same thing." This was Rashad talking. "Just 'cause she got that overwhelming urge to merge didn't mean you had to accommodate her. I know you've been with her X amount of years, but seeing a woman ain't like a job—you get no credit toward a pension for the time put in. I'm not saying you shouldn't have hit her off with the ring, I just hate hearing men sounding and acting all obligated. It all should come smooth and easy like Allan Houston's J."

For over a decade I'd been sitting in section 219 watching

the Knicks as fall flowed into winter and finally gave way to spring. David and Rashad had been sitting in this section for years. In between baskets and beer runs, this Odd Couple acted like a multiracial tag team with their rambling, always contradictory, advice.

David was an assistant D.A. in the Bronx who'd been born and raised in the city's northernmost (and most maligned) borough, yet maintained a certain bemused optimism toward life. Rashad was a sanitation department supervisor from Flushing who'd played high school ball and saw the dark side of most situations. Both were married with college-age kids, and their season tickets were the harshest vices in their admirably straight and narrow lives. Other than giving me advice on my love life and bugging me for the juicy details, talking about the Knicks was the glue that held together our three otherwise entirely different lives.

"Yeah," I replied, "well, all that's moot, Rashad. Millie and I are engaged. It's gonna happen and I'm happy about it. The only thing that worries me is why I waited so long to give her the ring. It's like I wanted her to react that way. I don't know why I did that."

"You're making too much of that, Dean." It was David again. He paused to drag on his beer and then continued. "She grows up dreaming about her wedding day. Dreaming of being a mother. Dreaming of a man fitting certain specifications. She was already in an expecting mood—that's all."

"Women," Rashad interjected, "spend too much time fantasizing and not enough in reality. Their expectations are their problem. Crying. Screaming. Fucking. They all the same thing, holmes. Manipulation and shit."

"That's true," David said, nodding his head in agreement.

Both my Knicks game pals were older, more experienced men. Yet they dismissed my uneasiness with a flick of their collective tongues. Maybe they were right. Maybe I was being too sensitive. Maybe my quiet joy at Millie's tears was just part of commitment. I manipulate her; she manipulates me. Bottom line was we were engaged. I'd crossed that river and, ultimately, wasn't that what really mattered?

Our attention turned from my love life to the basketball court below. The Miami Heat were taking the floor, with slick-haired Pat Riley leading the way.

While I'd been happily obligated to talk about my engagement to Millie—they knew my plan for that weekend as well as I did—I'd held back on mentioning Bee. It was all too freaky, too dramatic and too threatening to my relationship with Millie for quick conversation at a ball game. Both David and Rashad had teased me about the bold Pucci tie I was sporting—that gift for who I could become—and I told them it was from Millie, which smoothed that out.

Still, and as subtly as possible, I used David's binoculars to scan the crowd for Bee. As David and Rashad rattled on in the first quarter about the Knick offensive scheme and how Riley's wardrobe was falling off, I worked the room with my eyes, anxious for a glimpse of Bee's sassy walk and striking face.

Midway through the second quarter I'd given up and handed David back his toy. Whatever her game was, I'd fallen for it. Instead of watching a spirited battle between two evenly matched clubs, I'd been wasting time on a mind game I couldn't win. I was ordering a hot dog when David went, "Well, well, well."

"Whatcha got?" Rashad asked.

"Coming down the ramp directly across." David leered as he handed Rashad the binoculars. Rashad took a second to follow David's instructions and then grinned lecherously.

"Sexy, sexy, sexy," he muttered.

There was no need for me to grab the binoculars. Across thousands of fans and vendors, across a basketball court and two dozen millionaire athletes, across the world's most famous arena, there was no mistaking Bee's strut. Especially since those firm, shapely legs and that strong, fine figure were wrapped in a dress the hot red of a rapidly beating heart.

"I know her."

"Stop lying," Rashad said.

"No," I insisted, "its true. Her name's Bee Cole."

"Well," David announced in a dry tone, "she doesn't look cold to me."

Guided by a most courteous usher, Bee sat in the VIP section two rows behind Spike Lee and his lovely wife, Tanya. Though the game was intense, there'd been a low audible murmur as Bee worked her way to her seat—it was as if her strut was causing aftershocks.

"I have to talk to her."

"You mean," David said, "you want to talk to her."

"No." I stood up. "I have to."

I was waiting for Rashad to make some snide comment, but he just looked at me and then turned his gaze back toward Bee.

Getting courtside is never easy at the Garden, but just as I was exiting our section the half-time buzzer sounded, sending thousands of fans to the restrooms, concession stands and phone booths, creating a thundering human obstacle course.

I felt like I'd suddenly been dropped into an action flick where I had to navigate a minefield to save my lady.

I tried to keep my eyes peeled on Bee, who, at first, sat placidly in her chair. Yet the closer I got, the more agitated she seemed. Maybe I was projecting my anxiety into her, but Bee seemed to be looking around, scanning the crowd for me just as I had done earlier for her.

I was just one level above her and one section away when a red-jacketed usher blocked my path. "Ticket please," he requested. The usher's job was to make it difficult to enter the charmed section of courtside seats and, usually, I could penetrate this area with the right face and body language. But my eagerness betrayed me. I didn't look like I belonged there because I was too anxious to get in.

Over his shoulder I could see Bee standing up and the man next to her—a white man in a well-cut business suit—eyeing her approvingly.

I tried to move past the usher, who now eyed me with vigilant vigor. "Move on, buddy," he growled. A security guard in a blue blazer and a very serious scowl came up behind me and bellowed, "What? We got a situation here?"

Before things got ugly, I moved on. There was another, longer way around and I took it. This route would take me across a long aisle, down steps and under the seats. As I walked, I kept glancing over my shoulder toward Bee, trying to will her to wait for me.

Not only was this frustrating, but it was embarrassing. Up in section 219 I knew David and Rashad were tracking me, trying hard not to be sarcastic and unsympathetic, and failing miserably. I knew they'd be doing what I'd do—shifting their eyes from me to Bee and back again, as if in a movie, except a happy ending wasn't preordained. Besides, even I, the protagonist of the piece, wasn't sure if this was a tragedy or comedy.

So I concentrated on maneuvering around the strolling fans, the vendors and the restroom lines. There was one more checkpoint before I reached courtside, and an elderly usher with thick bifocals manned it. I was planning my strategy when someone pinched my ass. It was a firm two-fingered squeeze of my right buttock, which made me turn quickly. Standing in prime pinching position were two white businessmen sipping beer and talking Little League baseball. For a moment I wondered if these were gay men disguised under a very effective cloak of suburban normalcy.

Then, to my left, a woman laughed and announced, "Surprisingly firm, Dean Chance."

Bee stood there, basking in my embarrassment. And then she took my hand and led me out of the main room past the usher, a concession line and a popcorn vendor. Now, in the hallway, the low half-time hum of the Garden began to fade. In fact, our walk was almost soundless. It was as if all the human energy in the building was muffled simply by touching Bee's soft palm. Yes, we were still inside the world's most famous arena, but now separated from the crowd by a cocoon of Bee's creation.

We glided down a wide corridor past restrooms, whizzed by the security guards outside the Knicks locker room and a bank of Verizon pay phones. We went outdoors to an empty hallway where there were escalators and windows that looked down on Eighth Avenue. "Let's go," she said. I didn't argue.

Chapter 8

Her driver was waiting down by the entrance where the Garden gives way to Penn Station. He smiled knowingly when he saw me and then wordlessly walked us over to where the sedan was illegally parked. We headed up Eighth Avenue as Theolonious Monk's "Straight, No Chaser" filled the car. A mini–TV screen built into the back of both front seats played the Knicks–Heat game, but Spree couldn't lure my attention away from Bee.

Bee didn't watch the game either. Nor, however, did she look my way. Instead she leaned back and looked out the tinted windows at the passing cityscape. Yes, our shoes were off, but our toes weren't touching. She seemed tired. "Long day?" I asked as we crossed Columbus Circle and continued up Central Park West.

"A normal day," she replied to the window. Then she turned toward me and smiled. "Don't worry. I'm not ready to sleep, Dean. We're almost there." Then, without commenting, she touched the Pucci tie I was wearing. I waited for her to say something. She just fondled it and let it go.

The car pulled up in front of a building on Sixty-seventh

Street between Columbus and Broadway, a recent, tall, expensive contribution to the West Side skyline. The lobby had dark, burnished wood walls, a nodding doorman named Ramon and the feel of a place where swanky folk spent money easily.

"You nervous, Dean?" she asked in the elevator. Her eyes were alive again, her manner assertive and teasing. Wherever Bee had gone during the ride, she'd returned.

"Should I be?"

"Strange woman. Strange place. You don't know what I'm capable of."

"Then maybe I should go back downstairs and catch a cab back to the Garden. I'm sure I could catch the fourth quarter."

The elevator stopped on the thirty-third floor and the doors slid open. "Maybe you should," she replied and got off the elevator. In my mind I envisioned a simple, almost heroic series of events: I stay on the elevator, go back to the Garden and, when I get home, call the woman I love. All I had to do was stand there and let the doors close. In fact, the doors were already sliding shut when I pressed the "Open" button. The elevator buzzed defiantly a moment and then the doors separated. Bee hadn't broken her stride or looked back. I headed down the hall behind her to apartment 33C. Strange woman. Strange place. Excited me.

The living room was long and wide and sunken. I stepped down into a thick, cushy rust-colored rug ringed by two halves of a long, circular sofa of the same shade. In fact, the whole space had the color of good Hennessy. Around the room were tiny lit red candles. The only bright light in the room was aimed gallery-style at a huge photo that dominated the far wall.

A basketball, majestic and alone, hung in the air of some sports arena. Below it were hands—long, brown, grasping, anxious—all climbing atop each other as if the ball were desire itself. "I know you like basketball, Bee, but this seems a strange photo to see in a woman's place."

From behind me Bee replied, "To me that photo is about more than basketball. It represents a way of looking at the world. Rebounding, like life, is about control. Everybody fighting to position themselves—shoving, grabbing, pushing. In the end, one person gets the ball, because it's got to come down, Dean." She was standing beside me now, her shoulder rubbing lightly against my arm. "Somebody ends up in control—but never for very long. The balance shifts. The ball comes down somewhere else. No one's in control all the time. But some people—some people never are. Ever wonder when you'll be in control?"

"Every damn day," I said.

"Is that your only thought on it? You worry about it but have no plan?"

"Well, judging by how we met, letting someone else run things is sometimes a good idea."

"Is it that simple for you, Dean? You can let go that easily?"

Now we were facing each other, her eyes probing me. I felt like I was on trial. If Bee judged my reply silly, stupid or corny, I knew I'd be back on the elevator, heading down thirty-three frustrating floors. And that, actually, would have been for the best. I'd done nothing fatally wrong yet. But I wanted Bee and that desire overpowered my obligations and judgment. Lust had toppled many empires—so I guess my fall would be no big deal. I said, "Okay, it's not that easy to give up control." Bee didn't reply, as if she was waiting for more.

"But then," I added, "it's not always fun being in control, 'cause it means you have to make choices."

Bee touched my arms with her hands, squeezing them as she inquired, "And you don't want to do that, right?"

"Not all the time," I answered.

"I do." Now her hands held my waist and slid down to my hips. Her touch was firm, almost masculine.

"No surprise there," I said, though it was becoming very difficult for me to speak.

"But, you know," she said, "so far in our young relationship, you have had all the control."

I forced a laugh out of my constricted throat and told her, "You're crazy. Like in that old Spike Lee movie, I've been 'a mere lump of clay' for you."

"Oh, no, you're wrong," she chided me. "It's you who chose the tie. It's you who got in my ride. And you chose to come here tonight. In every case, all I did was offer. It's been your choice, Dean. So who's in control—you or me?"

Though we were so close I could feel her breathe, I still didn't touch her. Maybe if I didn't make a move her spell would be broken and I could still, even at this intimate moment, escape my bad intentions.

"How," I asked, "does a little girl with a nice mommy and daddy get to be you?"

Bee reached up to my neck and began removing my (her) tie. "That's an easy question to answer, Dean—I'm man-made."

She slid the tie from my neck and turned away. She walked across the thick carpet and, with a wiggle, a tug and a shimmy, slipped out of that fire truck of a dress, revealing a matching red bra, panties and an old-fashioned garter belt. Then she turned and faced me, wrapping that Pucci tie around her neck. With her look alone—no words, no gestures—Bee led me toward the bedroom like I was a hungry puppy.

The bedroom was the same warm rusty color as the living room. She turned to face me and began removing the last of her undergarments. I stood before her and did the same, taking off my clothes while never removing my eyes from hers. For a moment we stood still, as if awaiting a signal. I guess I heard it first because I was suddenly panting like an animal, sucking and biting her flesh in a feeding frenzy.

I was so hot for this woman I damn near came on her belly. Bee, however, changed the tempo. "No," she said, stopping me from entering her. I was about to grab Trojans from my pants when, from somewhere under the bed covers, Bee pulled out two sets of handcuffs. She handed them to me. I looked at them a moment, giddy and nervous.

"If you can't figure out how to use them," she said petulantly, "I'll take them back."

Anger flashed through me. I decided to take command. With one set, I cuffed Bee's hands in front of her as if she were a felon being led into court. Then stood with the other set of cuffs, looking into Bee's eyes as I awaited instructions.

"Use your imagination, Dean." She spoke it like a challenge, one intensified by that hot/cold smile of hers. So I cuffed her feet together. Now what? Bee lifted the tie from the carpet with her cuffed hands and licked it. Her eyes were like fireflies. "Put it around my eyes." An order spoken like a request. If this had been Millie, I would already have wrapped her up like a package, but Bee was directing and it felt right.

Her next words were "Reach under the bed." Custom condoms, I thought. A nice big box of them. But there was no condom box. There was no white and green package. What I touched was long, hard and had a brown carved handle. "Pull it out," she said. "Come on." Even though she was blindfolded, I knew Bee could feel my shock. She'd anticipated my uneasiness and was pleased by it.

The knife had a smooth, lean handle, was slender as a straw and as long as my size-twelve shoes. It caught the light from the high-rise across the street and gleamed like a Porsche on Broadway. I noticed that the windows were open and faced the opposing building. "Do you want me to close the window?"

"Dean," she replied, ignoring my query, "I want you to use the blade."

It looked good up against her shoulders, her arms and then around her lovely navel. I laid the tip against the inside of her navel and she shuddered.

"Say my name," I ordered, not because I necessarily wanted to hear her go through this tired sexual ritual, but because I had no idea what to do next.

"Dean," she replied for me.

"Say my whole name."

"Dean Chance."

I put my ear to her lips as I continued to rub the blade against her belly and her arms. I whispered, "Say my name. Say it real sweet and low, real sweet and low."

But instead of following my shaky script, Bee improvised. "Are you going to hurt me now?"

Hell no, I thought, but I did lay the point against one brown nipple and then the other. I felt edgy and in command now. I was suddenly liking the whole scene. Then Bee hissed, "Cut me," and my body stiffened.

"Who's in control, Dean? Whose choice is it?" Okay, I thought, and I nicked her on the right shoulder with the tip and an inky drop of blood popped out of her skin. I licked the wound clean and then started biting her neck like it was candy. My teeth made Bee moan—loud and crazy, like I'd never heard anyone in my whole entire life.

Now I flipped her over, ass up on the bed, smacked that behind like I was insulted and then slipped on my Trojan. I pulled her cheeks and legs wide apart with my hands and then slid into her. She was so sweet I thought my poor dick was gonna drown. Later I'd make her give it mouth-to-mouth resuscitation, but right now I was just answering her question of control with every stroke.

Chapter 9

A cool breeze blew in through the open window and dried the moisture on my chest. My stomach growled and I looked over at my still-shackled bedmate. "You want to take those off?" Her half-opened eyes widened and she said, "No," before turning away from me.

So, buck-naked and hazy, I wandered back out into the living room, gazing for a moment at the hands wrestling for control before entering the kitchen. Unlike the rest of Bee's apartment, this room was sleek and cold, with a big metal refrigerator and matching chrome fixtures. Inside of the fridge: bottles of soda, beer and water. No meat. No fruit. No vegetables. No milk. Nothing half-empty.

The fridge was full but somehow unlived in. The freezer was empty except for some ice racks. I started opening cabinets. The first was empty. So were the next and the next. In the last cabinet I found an unopened bag of potato chips. Did she really live here or was this just a very expensive flophouse?

Back in the living room I spotted a videocassette and a remote on the floor. The remote was one of those complicated multi-use numbers but, after some trial and error, I got the thing going and a wall rolled up to reveal a state-of-the-art home entertainment system—flat TV, DVD, VCR, stereo, the works. I walked over to the VCR and stuck the tape in.

The screen filled with soundless footage of a music video. Time-code numbers at the bottom. Scantily clad dancers gyrating. Some bare-chested male singer lounging in leopard pants. I got so engrossed in the footage I didn't notice Bee coming up behind me. Suddenly my clothes were on my head.

Pulling my drawers off my face, I saw Bee, fully dressed and slightly irritated. She took the remote from me and clicked off the footage.

"Are we leaving?"

"I have to get to a meeting, Dean." I was getting shown the door. Trying to salvage some dignity, I responded, "Shit, it must be midnight. What kind of meeting could you be having now?"

"That's my business. All you need to know is that I have to go and so do you."

"Are you going to give me your number?" I knew I sounded like a sucker, but hell, I couldn't help it.

"Thought you'd ask."

Bee pulled a business card out of her purse. An engraved letter *B* and a cell phone number.

"Staying mysterious, huh?"

"That's who I am, sweetcakes." She came over and patted my cheek with her hand. "Now get dressed."

Out on Sixty-seventh Street the driver stood by the car, puffing on what smelled like a Cuban. I searched his face for a smile, a smirk or some wry amusement. He gave me nothing. He just carefully put out his smoke and opened the door for Bee. Before I could stop myself, I uttered a true sucker's last words: "When will I see you again?"

"Soon," Bee said suavely.

"You haven't just played me, have you?" That was real weak, so I came back with "If you have, it's been fun. Can't say it hasn't. But if you're through, just do me in now and don't keep me hoping."

"You sure are anxious, sweetcakes."

"Dean. Dean Chance. Remember?"

"I won't play you, Dean. But I will play with you again."

Bee kissed me softly and then squeezed my butt. "Gotta go." She slid into the back; the driver closed the door and moved to the driver's seat. Bee rolled down the window and said, "Keep my shit tight, a'ight?"

As the car pulled off, through the open window I could see Bee writing in her Palm Pilot. I was watching the car cross Broadway when I felt this chill. It was spring in New York. Sixty degrees. A hint of summer dancing in the air. Yet I found myself a bit cold. Maybe because I'd cheated so willingly on my fiancée. Perhaps because Bee had freaked me so completely. Either way it was time to go home.

FROM: COLDB@HOTMAIL.COM

TO: SEECEE@HOTMAIL.COM

SUBJECT: RIGHT & WRONG

It happened. You were right and, as always, you were also wrong. Yes, I was able to seduce him. But no, and I'm sure this will upset you, he was QUITE entertaining in the sack. Sorry about that.

FROM: SEECEE@HOTMAIL.COM

TO: COLDB@HOTMAIL.COM

SUBJECT: RE: RIGHT & WRONG

How are your wrists and ankles? Still sore? Or have you finally gotten used to the rubbing after all this time?

FROM: COLDB@HOTMAIL.COM

TO: SEECEE@HOTMAIL.COM

SUBJECT: RE(2): RIGHT & WRONG

You bastard! Are you spying on me again? I try to open up a line of communication with you and you violate our agreement over and over. I don't think this is gonna work, so leave me the fuck alone!

FROM: SEECEE@HOTMAIL.COM

TO: COLDB@HOTMAIL.COM

SUBJECT: YOU & ME

How could I ever do that? I've never met a woman like you. Never had a relationship like ours. It's not that I haven't tried to replace you. But I believe now that that's impossible. Leave you alone? Okay, but only when you stop haunting me!

Chapter 10

―――――― ⁊ ――――――

The new Times Square turns some people off. Those nostalgic for the gritty, funky flavor of the past complain that the blocks from Forty-second to Fiftieth on Broadway and Seventh are as antiseptic and tourist friendly as a strip mall. But those people aren't looking closely. There are still young people wandering the streets who really belong in school. You still get offered stolen goods. Keep your eyes too wide open looking at the TV screens and the neon lights and your pocket will be picked. And sex, more subterranean perhaps, is still available—both the free and the professional kind.

I was inside the Virgin Megastore on Seventh Avenue, which was one of the first destination retailers to open and revitalize Times Square. With its loud music, flashing lights and heady atmosphere of nonstop commerce, this three-level retail outlet has the same kinetic atmosphere as the streets outside. Not that I'm a regular shopper here. Whenever I do find myself here, though, I head right down the escalator to the jazz section. I usually don't wander the place, because pop music is not my addiction. Miles, Monk and Trane are my usual fix. But on this day I circled the top floor, half looking at the rows of CDs and half admiring my assistant's perky butt as she strolled ahead of me. "What's the latest, greatest thing happening in the twenty-first century, Tanya?"

"Depends on what kind of music you like, Dean."

"The youngest musician in my collection is Roy Hargrove and he's probably got gray in his braids by now. You're going to have to give me a little more guidance."

"Well, maybe we should just buy you a copy of every CD in the top ten and go from there."

Tanya had on shiny knee-high black boots, a hot-pink summer dress and a matching pink barrette in her short, bobbed hair. Under her arm was a leopard handbag. She struck me as totally contemporary and totally cute.

"You going out tonight, Tanya?"

"Yeah. A couple of girlfriends and I are going to this new club in Chelsea. You're welcome to join us. Might be good research."

A tempting offer but I was already in enough trouble with Bee in my life, so I said, "I think I'll take the CDs we buy home and tend to my studies." We passed a magazine rack and I bent down to scoop up a *Billboard*, *Rolling Stone*, *Vibe* and *Source*.

Tanya said, "Dean, if you really wanna catch up on what's current, what you need to do is sit up and watch music videos. You'll get the music, the clothes, the style, everything."

"Well," I said sheepishly, "I hate most music videos. I mean, if I wanna watch porno, I'll watch porno. I see those girls shaking their butts and I wonder what does that have to do with music? It's just some pimply, tattooed singer getting his rocks off. To me, videos devalue music."

Tanya smiled and spoke with youthful condescension. "I understand what you're saying, Dean, but videos are the quickest way to catch up."

Right in front of us was a huge in-store video screen. I peered up at it and saw Maxwell, the epitome of fashion-model soul, crooning to a leggy sister with curly, streaked blond hair. Her body was divine and her face a confusion of beauty, like she had so many beauty genes her DNA couldn't decide what kind of fine she should be. "I think I know that girl," I said under my breath.

Tanya said, "Then you must be looking at more videos than you admit to, since she's the video 'It girl' of the moment."

"I don't think it's from a video, Tanya."

"From a dream maybe?" Tanya was now teasing my horny ass, so I played along.

"Yeah, a wet one."

"Calm down, Dean."

"I'm joking."

"I know you are, Mr. Engaged."

Despite Tanya's well-aimed barb, I stood staring at the screen, squeezing my brain for a memory until this video vision came alive. That day on Central Park West with Millie—she was the taller of the two girls inhaling tongue that afternoon. As she danced around Maxwell, I remembered her and I smiled. Like Robin Harris used to say, "Small world."

FROM: ALADY27@EARTHLINK.NET

TO: SEECEE@HOTMAIL.COM

SUBJECT: OUR RELATIONSHIP

You impress me. You seem to know so much about other people's desires; it's as if you've done everything yourself. It's possible, I guess, but seems awfully tiring. Between my work, my man and plain old moving from one place to another, sex is a wonderful but not an all-encompassing part of my life. I guess that's why I watch. It's sex a step removed. I learn about the world but don't have to take a shower afterward. I know to someone like you it sounds like a dodge, but it's what makes me comfortable.

FROM: SEECEE@HOTMAIL.COM

TO: ALADY27@EARTHLINK.NET

SUBJECT: YOUR ROAD

I hope you don't feel that I am in any way judging you. I do not judge. Judging people's sexual appetites is for Republican Congressmen and talk show audiences. My philosophy, which you should know by now, is that all of us—you, me, whoever—could go farther and enjoy more. I know you are capable of other, more engaged sexual experiences. I believe I am just a road you're traveling to get there. There's a rainbow out there for you, Dorothy. I just wanna be there when you reach it.

Chapter 11

Three days later. Another Knicks game. First quarter. Michael Jordan's Washington Wizards are in town, but me and the boys in section 219 are focused on other things.

"So," David said, "sum it up for us, Dean."

"She owns or has access to a slick apartment in the West Sixties."

"So she's wealthy."

"Or," Rashad interjected, "he has bank. 'He' being (a) the fool she lives with, (b) the sucker she's married to, (c) the motherfucker who's keeping her."

"She has rough cuts of music videos in the apartment."

"So," David picked up, "she works in that industry—a director, a producer, an executive of some kind. Or maybe she's in advertising."

"Or," Rashad interjected, "the pro ball–playing nigga payin' the bills is into all that."

"She left around midnight—said she was going to a meeting."

"I'm telling you, Dean, she's sucking dick to pay the bills." This was Rashad.

David countered, "Not necessarily. People in the entertainment business keep unconventional hours."

"Well," I said, "I can testify that that's right. It would also explain being free to shop during the afternoon."

"She's being kept, Money," Rashad said roughly.

"Or she works nights on lucrative productions," David came back with.

"She has access to great Knicks tickets," David observed. "They could be hers, a man's or the company's she works for."

Rashad asked, "What about the G that drives her?"

"He's definitely the bodyguard type. I got the feeling he's strapped. He makes me feel like she needs protection. Maybe from a man. Maybe from real thugs. She could be in the drug game, though I don't think so."

"In other words," Rashad said in summation, "you really don't know shit about her."

"Excuse me." At the end of the row was that mean-ass usher from the other night. Tonight he wore the tight good humor of a man suddenly well paid. "You Dean Chance?" I told him the truth.

"What?" Rashad wondered. "Is he getting something free? Or getting moved down? 'Cause if he is, I'm Dean Chance."

The usher passed down an envelope, saying, "It didn't look free to me," with a smile.

With David and Rashad at full attention, I opened the envelope. Inside was a flyer for the Paradise Gentlemen's Club. On the back, written in red lipstick, were the words "Tip Well."

"Who gave this to you?

The usher laughed. "I was told to tell you my supervisor, but only a mammoth bottle of gin would make me mistake your friend for Joe Fitzgerald. I'd wish you luck, but you clearly don't need any, buddy."

As the usher headed back down the steps, David peered through his binoculars toward courtside. "I don't see her, Dean, but who else could it be from?"

"Well, I'll see," I said, somewhat embarrassed about this sudden attention.

"Mind if I join you?" It was David.

"I thought you had a sweet little woman waiting at home for you?"

"I do. I do. But a man can dream, can't he?"

Rashad laughed derisively. "Dream? Motherfucker, you don't go to a strip club to dream. If that's what you're gonna do, keep your dead ass home. That's not what me and Dean are planning. Are we, Dean?"

Impressed by his illogic, all I could say was, "I guess not."

I managed to keep my two friends seated until late in the fourth quarter when Sprewell drove the lane for a game-winning bucket. With the game in hand, Rashad and David hustled me out onto Seventh Avenue and east on Thirty-third Street across Herald Square to the Gentlemen's Paradise Club. Due to its location in a busy retail district (and away from schools and churches), the Paradise had survived the infamous late-nineties Giuliani strip club purge. Prosperous and relatively discreet, the Paradise had serviced Knicks and Ranger fans for years.

A big Latino in a tight suit and slicked-back hair stood

behind a podium just inside the door. "Good evening, gentlemen," he said professionally. "Welcome to the Paradise Club. It's twenty dollars at the door. Half price if you have Knicks tickets."

"Which we do," David said with unnecessary defiance.

"Well, then," the doorman said, quite amused, "let's see them."

As we paid, I asked, "Excuse me—is Bee working tonight?"

The doorman's amusement evolved into a full-fledged smile. "So, you're looking for Bee, huh? Alright, my lucky man, I'll tell her you're here. In the meantime, you and your friends go in and relax. Have a drink. Tip one of our fine young ladies."

As we walked in I could feel the doorman sizing me up and I got that chill again.

At David's insistence we sat right in front of the long stage and quickly ordered overpriced drinks. Strip clubs actually have never done much for me. Too fake, too mechanical, too rote. I admire the bodies, maybe tip one or two. But instead of getting me hot, I get bored. I hoped my erotic senses wouldn't be too dulled by the time Bee revealed herself.

Rashad was a man in his element—flirting with the dancers, telling nasty jokes, acting as if the entire club had been designed for his comfort. David's eyes were wide as a child's on Christmas morning. This was a man who definitely kept things under wraps—suppressing his lust to keep house and home stable. I worried about him and he was likely worried about himself. A couple of times I heard him mumble, "I really need to start back home," but he didn't move a muscle. Then this hugely endowed short blonde sauntered over in five-inch heels and thrust her lungs his way. He pushed a five-dollar donation between her breasts and unleashed a gasp of joy not heard from David since Larry Johnson's four-point play in 'ninety-nine.

When the blonde had moved on, David said, "God, the wife's gonna be worried."

"No," Rashad said, "she's gonna be happy 'cause you're coming home with the hardest dick she's seen in years." I had to join Rashad in laughing at David, but our happily married friend was above all that now. He just waved over another girl and suggested, "We should do this after every game, guys."

"Shit, David," Rashad said with sudden wisdom, "we already spent our lunch money for the tickets. We're spending our retirement money right now."

"Rashad," David countered, "I've been to Florida—this is better."

"Just shows you," Rashad said. "Behind every reasonable man is a freak. Just like our young friend here."

"You talking to me?"

"No, Dean, I'm talking about you."

The doorman came up behind me and bent down. "Gentlemen, follow me," he said.

"Gentlemen? What do you mean, gentlemen? You mean me, right?"

"You want to see Bee," he replied. "She wants to see you. And them too."

Before I could utter another word of protest, my pals were standing up, more than ready for whatever came next.

"Lead the way, sir," David said happily.

"Yeah," Rashad agreed, "let's get this party started quickly."

We were led down a staircase into a dim corridor illuminated by hot blue neon lights that reflected off the floor-to-ceiling mirrors. On either side of the corridor were many doors—all of them closed save one at the end of the hall. The doorman guided us into a room that had a faux-African theme, with tiger murals and stools designed to look like drums. West African dance music flirted through the speakers. The three of us sat on the leopard-print sofa—silent, staring straight ahead.

Finally Rashad turned to me. "Relax, man, we're just gonna watch."

"Yeah, " David chimed in, "we're just interested observers."

The lights dimmed a bit and the door opened and Bee entered, garbed in tiny strips of leopard fabric that covered but didn't conceal her taut body. Her eye makeup was extreme, like she'd just come in from the road company of *Cats.*

"Damn!" This was Rashad on my right. The guttural groan to my left was David.

I stood up. "What's this all about, Bee?"

She danced over toward me, her hips swaying and her eyes bearing down on me. "No show works without an audience," she whispered. She then stepped back to the center of the room and began to dance for David and Rashad. As you might imagine, the two old codgers were highly entertained. David pulled a twenty-dollar bill out of his wallet and offered it to her. She glided over to him and let him stick the bill into the leopard fabric covering her groin.

That was it. I didn't think. I didn't say anything. I just walked out of the faux-African room and into the neon corridor. I took maybe three strides before the doorman blocked my way. "Is there a problem, sir?"

"Yeah, motherfucker, there's a problem."

He laughed and said, "Bee thought there might be."

"Did she? Well, she was right." I tried to move around him but he wouldn't accommodate me.

"If I were you," he suggested calmly, "I'd go back in. Why would you wanna upset a woman like that?"

Bee's voice—laughing joyfully—emanated from the faux-African room. The doorman raised an eyebrow. Curious and furious, I turned around and yanked open the half-closed door. "What the fuck?!"

Bee was on the leopard sofa, laughing, with a fifty-dollar bill in each hand. David and Rashad, shorn of all their dignity and most of their clothes, danced to African music for her entertainment. It was the funniest thing I'd seen in years. Rashad and David wiggled their old asses as shamelessly as real strippers, while Bee fanned herself with the fifties.

"The champagne's coming, Dean," she said. "Care to join us?"

FROM: SEECEE@HOTMAIL.COM

TO: ALADY27@EARTHLINK.NET

SUBJECT: MY WORK

They used to say watching pornography was for men. They used to say that women didn't respond to the objectification of human bodies as men do. You and I know better. This bit of footage is different from the others I send you. No more professionals. I am the star here. Hope you enjoy my performance.

FROM: ALADY27@EARTHLINK.NET

TO: SEECEE@HOTMAIL.COM

SUBJECT: YOUR WORK

Well, I don't know what to say. That was amazing. You were quite impressive, but who were those two women? They seemed quite familiar with you and each other. I knew there was more to you than meets the eye. Now I know how much more.

Chapter 12

There is no normal. There is no ordinary. There is only your imagination, your desires, your naked urges unencumbered by rules or laws. Bonds weren't broken. They just disappeared in the matrix of Bee's body. When Bee took me, everything outside the room evaporated. My bosses, the network, my woman, my bank account, my family and every one of the other boxes that squeezed my soul didn't matter when I entered Bee.

Sex with Bee was like a scream I've been holding inside since my baby-sitter's ass made my nature rise at age seven. I've wanted to scream like this forever and, every now and then, it's flown from my lips with other women. My dear Millie has elicited it once or twice.

But Bee made me whine like a cat in heat just by a touch on my hand. She reached into me and yanked out the inner workings so that my insides lay on the bed beside my skin, all of me exposed, all of me quivering, all of me—inside, outside, soul, intellect—screaming, screaming, screaming.

Bee didn't make the earth move. When I was with Bee there was no earth.

It was hours after the game and the strip club and all that drama. The apartment. The bedroom. The curtains open again. No handcuffs, though. Just old-school sexing. Bee lay atop me, her head on my chest, staring at my half-opened eyes as sweat dripped from her forehead.

"I made a good choice this time," she said softly.

"Did you?"

"Oh, yes. You're proving to be quite a good sport."

"I could still mess up."

"As long as you don't go psycho on me, we'll be fine, Dean. 'Cause you will mess up—it's what people do."

"Sounds like you know about that. But considering your taste in jokes, it ain't a surprise."

Bee rolled over on her back and stared up at the ceiling. "Remember," she asked, "when you asked how I got this way?"

"Sure."

"There was a man," she began dreamily. "He opened me up. Turned me into a flower—made me blossom."

"So," I said, holding that word for a long time. "Where is he now?"

"You sound jealous."

"I'm not jealous," I lied. "Just curious."

"Curious because you're jealous."

"You're the one who should be jealous," I said, grasping for the upper hand. "I have a woman, you know?"

"And," she said quite happily, "I'm married."

Took me a minute to recover from that. "Okay, you topped me," I finally replied. "So right now you're committing adultery."

"One of my many sins, Dean."

"So your husband is who turned you out?"

"So far out that when I looked in the mirror I could see my liver, my spleen and my big red heart." This made her laugh and me nervous.

"Why am I here, then?"

"I love an insecure man."

"I'm leaving."

"Alright, Dean, go."

I pushed myself out of bed and searched for my underwear in the bed's tangled sheets. Finding it at the foot of the bed, I then turned my attention to finding my pants. Bee sat up and watched me with a smirk.

"But if you leave now, Dean, you'll never hear the rest of my story. It's rare that I'm this open. Once the mood passes . . ." She had me and she knew it. I took a seat on the edge of the bed. "Okay," I said. "Let's go back to my question—the one I asked before I sounded insecure. Where is he?"

"Oh, he's around. Which is why I have Evander—my driver—watching my back. We're legally separated—and will someday soon be officially divorced. Anything else you probably would like to know?"

"Now, that's funny," I said. "This is the first bit of personal info you've given up. There's a lot I would like to know."

"Well, there is something you need to know," she said slowly. "He might be following you."

"Is he dangerous?"

"Not to you," she said. "Not physically. But Christian is a clever man. He observes people—knows how to see into them and bring things out you'd never imagine were inside. When we got married it was as if I'd joined the circus, a place where you did things you never thought you could. My husband was a magician and I was his apprentice. The thing is his magic wears out. I woke up from his illusion one morning and I haven't gone back—though obviously the effects of his tricks haven't worn off."

"Am I going to wake up real soon desperate to cleanse my soul?"

"You might," she said with a giggle. "I mean, your Millie will be back soon. Everything could change the minute you see her. After all, you are engaged."

Bee headed into the bathroom. I sat there as the sound of the shower filled my ears. I walked over to the window and looked at the city. Satisfied yet unsettled too. I realized I was in over my head with Bee but happy about it. Bee gave me naturally what I manufactured with Millie—surprise, shock and supple sensuality. But nothing in life was one-sided pleasure. There was always a flip side—another, sadder angle on whatever was going down.

And her ex was obviously it. A husband. A demon lover. A man who turns women out. That chill—that same one from the other nights with Bee—ran through me. But this was the coldest yet. I felt it right in my gut, like I'd discovered an ulcer. I pulled the curtains closed, as if there was a draft coming through the glass. But the only movement in that room was the churning inside me.

Chapter 13

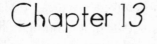

In a city where space is at a premium, it's rare to stand upon a bit of unessential New York real estate. Randall's Island is just such a hunk of earth. It sits in the East River, farther north than the efficient condos and neat streets of that yuppie island dubbed Roosevelt and south of that barbed and barbaric sliver of hell named Rikers.

On Randall's there are few citizens, law abiding or not, and no subway stations, twenty-four-hour supermarkets or video stores. The chief feature of this mostly empty and usually forgotten dirt patch is Downing Stadium, an unkempt, aging edifice that is the Apple's most unappealing concert venue. It's the place for concerts the Garden turns its nose up at— alternative rock festivals, Ecstasy-stoked raves and any events involving large, sweaty groups of shirtless white kids.

The isolation of Randall's Island is ensured by the limited means of access. The chief entrance to the place is one fairly narrow ramp way off the Triborough Bridge. Randall's is hard to get to and hard to get off of. Which makes it so ironic that city bus drivers love it so.

Freed from the choked avenues of Manhattan and the clogged boulevards of the other boroughs, Randall's has been a place where you could ramble (once you're there) and rumble, shifting gears on long transports and turning the wide wheels with an ease unimaginable in most parts of New York.

Perhaps because of these advantages Randall's Island had become home not simply to wanton rock gigs, but to one of Nick Shaw's favorite events—the annual Bus Rodeo. On a day of brilliant white sunlight, 146 bus drivers, plus honorary transit worker Nick Shaw, competed in a test of driving skills that had been going on since 1979. With protruding stomachs that pushed their blue MTA shirts forward and all manner of sunglasses, drivers from all five boroughs and every depot in the city strove to win a five hundred dollar savings bond and a chance to travel to a huge national competition in Orlando, Florida.

But why were Nick Shaw and I here in a Randall's Island parking lot watching empty forty-foot buses navigate plastic cones, barrels and the odd tennis ball on a lovely Sunday?

Well, Shaw's father had been a superintendent at the Flushing terminal in Queens, so he'd grown up around buses and bus driver culture, where over dinner people debated the relative merits of drivers from different boroughs. Conventional wisdom held that Manhattan drivers were the city's best because they shared the road with yellow cabs, bike messengers and midtown jaywalkers. Shaw, a product of working-class Queens, favored his home borough's drivers but, in general, had a fascination with anything involving the smell of diesel in the morning.

"Isn't this great?" he turned and said to me as he wheeled our bus in position for "Sandra's Run," in which a bus hits one hundred miles per hour on a straightaway and then has to downshift with a minimum of rubber burn.

"Great," I said as I grabbed a pole and wrapped a long rope-colored yoga strap Millie had given me around it. "This is just how I should be spending my free time."

Shaw laughed. "I know you love this, Dean. After all, it's in your blood as deep as it is in mine."

I forced a smile and replied, "I guess," softly. The sad truth was Shaw had a point. Just as he'd grown up around buses, to some degree, so had I. Where Shaw's father had a solid city job, my father and mother had both driven school buses throughout much of my childhood.

When I'd first come in for my job interview with Shaw, I (and probably he) had perceived it as an affirmative action courtesy call. I had started my career in African-American media (New York talk station WLIB, a stint with one-time Black Entertainment Television host Bev Smith) before going mainstream with CNBC and later *The Today Show*. I'd shown a knack not simply for booking good guests, but for preparing interviews with those one or two questions that turn a chat to real conversation.

Shaw, who was now gunning the bus engine like it was a Harley and cackling like Jack Nicholson in *Cuckoo's Nest*, had also worked his way up the media ranks, from consumer watchdog in Providence to morning-show host in D.C. There he managed the delicate balancing act of cracking jokes while discussing Bosnia and Columbine. That gift, along with his solid Irish-American looks, got him a shot at syndicated TV riches. In the wake of comedians and rappers having talk shows, why not give a smart white guy a shot?

So when I walked through his door that day three and a half years back, I figured Shaw would be looking for experienced backup—an ex-Oprah gal, a Geraldo renegade or a survivor of the late-night wars. The interview was going just alright until he asked me what my father did for a living. When I revealed that both my mother and father had driven school buses in Manhattan and Queens, his eyes lit up and our conversation went from the professional to personal, from polite to high-spirited reminiscence. Against the wishes of a few higher-ups, I got the gig as segment producer supervising the all-important pre-interviews with guests and the preparation of our genial host.

Which is how I ended up here, inside a forty-foot New York M14 bus, gearing up to go as fast and as straight as the talkative son of a supervisor could go. "Shouldn't we be shooting this for the show?" I asked as I strapped myself into a passenger seat.

"Some pleasures must be private to remain pure," he said over his shoulder, and then the white flag was lowered and we were off. It was a two-hundred-foot straightaway that challenged the driver in two ways—to cross the finish line at high speed and then to stop in a precise and timely manner. The trick of this event was that you were judged on the combined score—your high speed as clocked by a speed gun and your ability to keep the bus straight as you applied the brakes. Too fast and you couldn't stop in a line; too slow and your finish wouldn't impress the judges.

Shaw wasn't interested in the niceties. My boss was a speed junkie to the core, so he gunned the M14 bus like it was the little red Corvette he tooled around the Hamptons in. This is one reason we were one of the few New York–based talk shows to do intelligent (and high-rated) programs on the NASCAR circuit. So, with his Ray-Bans on Shaw gunned us past idled buses, spectators on blankets and judges squinting at stopwatches.

"This," Shaw shouted, "should be an Olympic sport!"

All I could think, as my body shook and my heart fluttered, was how much I must like my job.

Past the last cone he lightened up on the pedal. My jaw slackened and the grinding sound in my head quieted. I could hear and smell rubber burning. We came to a long, wobbly stop totally appropriate to Shaw's background as a talk-show host. When he'd finally stopped, I leaned forward and said, "I don't think we won, Nick."

"But isn't your heart pounding, Dean?"

"Oh, yeah."

"Well, what else did you want out of life?"

Afterward we sat in his convertible, sipped brews and ate sandwiches as bus drivers and their families strolled by. Occasionally someone would come by and ask for Shaw's autograph, which he gave graciously. "Cool day, huh?" he said as yet another bus sped between orange plastic cones.

"It's different," I said diplomatically. "There's no question that it's different from the world we live in."

"I know it's not the Knicks," said Shaw, "but I like unusual stuff, Dean. It can't all be the usual recreation. You gotta push the envelope a bit. Be open to new shit."

"If this rap is designed to make me happier about the change in the show's direction, don't bother. I'll do what you want to do."

"But you should enjoy it, Dean. I'm not saying we become *The Ricki Lake Show*. I'm just saying there's a place between Jenny Jones and Charlie Rose, and we can live there. We can do things that are tabloidy but with some wit, some style."

"So," I cut in, "you're saying we're pioneers?"

"When are you getting your own show, Dean? You are sure one lean mean talker, my friend. I'll be glad when your girl gets back. I notice you're about four degrees warmer when you're getting laid."

"I am a little edgy, huh?" I acknowledged.

"Like a blade, Dean. But I don't really mind. It keeps me from getting all soft and mushy—on air and off. Thanks for coming out here with me. I know it's goofy but sometimes making a bit of a fool out of yourself clears out a lot of tension."

I said, "I hear you," and leaned back, thinking of my new friend Bee.

Chapter 14

A nother warm night in Bee's rust-colored world—one in which I exposed not only my body, but also parts I didn't even know were visible. It started with me being cocky. "My woman never has to ask me what to do," I bragged in Bee's bedroom, naked and sipping some Hennessy XO. "And she sure doesn't tell me. I do what I think is right. She never complains."

"Is that right?" Bee said with nonchalant malice.

"That's right," I answered with the vehement slurring of an inebriated man. "I support her career totally. I wanna have kids with her and, as you now know firsthand, sex with me is da bomb. What else could a woman want?" My liquored-up logic seemed inescapable to me.

"Your problem isn't sex, Dean." She was walking around the bed in a red La Perla bra and no panties, while smoking a joint.

"Thank you," I replied with sloppy assurance.

"Your lack of imagination is your problem." Bee spoke with clinical precision, despite the marijuana. "You think just because a thing isn't asked for, it's not wanted. It's the person who doesn't ask, who doesn't know how to ask, who craves imagination the most."

"You are always trying to fuck with my head," I said accusingly.

"'Cause you're too limited. Where you see barriers, I see possibilities." Almost thoughtful, she added, "You could be so much more than you are. Your Millie knows that."

"Leave her out of this!" That cold smile appeared at my outburst. My anger always seemed to please her, like it made her blood sizzle.

"Millie knows but she just doesn't know how to say it." She sat on the edge of the bed and took a deep, final drag on what was now a roach. "You should let me get with your Millie. When I'm through with her, she'd know just how to deal with you."

"Are you a lesbo, baby?" I sat up and tried to sound attacking and mean. "Now, it's alright with me if you are, but—"

"But nothing. If I was simply lesbian, I wouldn't be wasting my time with you."

"Simply?" I replied. "Being a lesbian is simple?"

Bee leaned in toward me with a deadly serious stare. "If you take men out of a woman's life, everything she does gets easier. From getting a job to child rearing. No more stupid football stories. No more two-minute brothers. Ain't been a woman born who can't go more than two minutes."

"Must everything be a goddamn speech?"

"Sorry, baby," she said softly. "One and one does not always equal two with me."

"Okay. I'll make it easy for you. Have you ever kissed a woman?"

"Yes." A pause. "My mother."

"Have you ever screwed a woman?"

"Screwed?" This made her laugh at me, like I was a joke of some kind.

"Let's just get down to it. Have you ever eaten pussy?"

"That would make me a lesbian?"

"Ah, you won't answer," I said like I'd proved something. "That says it all."

Bee shook her head and told me, "I like you but you are such a damn baby. You know what you do with babies?" She didn't let me answer. "You discipline them. Dean, reach under the bed." I knew what was under there. I hesitated a minute. She just stood there and folded her arms under the bra. I pulled the long knife out and held it up. Bee took it from me, then ran her tongue across its length and pointed the tip at my nose. "Don't move," she ordered.

Bee went to a closet and came back with a little chest. Out of it she pulled a familiar item and tossed it to me. The clicking of the lock was a bit scary. So was the steel against the wrists. But that was nothing compared to the fear that ran through me when she turned the chest so I could look inside. Four knives were mounted in red velvet. Three had curves and little serrated edges. The biggest had a hook that would scare Tinkerbell. "Which," she wondered, "would you prefer, Dean? Use your imagination."

I stood up and walked right up to her and the chest of knives and told her, "I'm tired. I have to go to work early tomorrow, Bee. So put your toys away, little girl. I'm not playing anymore."

Or so I thought. Bee closed the chest. She stepped back

from me and said, "Fine," with childish petulance and walked out of the room. I sat back on the bed, looked around for my clothes and then gazed down at the handcuffs. For centuries black men have been forced to wear them. Back in the day, it was to keep us in slavery. These days they were part of an industry of incarceration where we were the products, beaten down by bad schools, racism and our own poor judgment.

I was a handcuff virgin. And with every move I made I felt the metal weighing against my wrists, rubbing my flesh raw, lightly stinging my bones. I had joined that long line of vulnerable brothers, all of them controlled by others—be they slaves, prisoners or playthings, like me.

"Bee," I said loudly, "I need the keys." I heard the front door close. "Bee! Bee!"

The living room was empty. The kitchen was empty. Soundless footage of a singer with chains locked around his waist, wrist and feet played on the television. He looked to be in supreme ecstasy—the confinement seeming to fuel his singing fervor. I spent the better part of two hours looking around the place for the keys and, with each minute, I felt less and less sure of myself and more and more helpless. The footage of the singer kept playing—there must have been hours of this fool writhing around, locked up in someone's fantasy of love.

Three hours later my cell phone rang. Bee identified herself with a self-satisfied "Hello" and I shouted, "Where the fuck are the keys?"

"Where do you want them to be?"

"In my goddamn hand."

The front door swung open. Bee in a long leather jacket. Her cell in her hand. She tossed the keys toward me and they landed at my feet.

"Why?" I asked.

"Use your imagination," she said and then closed the door.

FROM: ALADY27@EARTHLINK.NET

TO: SEECEE@HOTMAIL.COM

SUBJECT: THAT COUPLE

I LOVED THAT COUPLE! The way they used those toys on one another. They were sensitive to each other. It made me jealous. I want that level of communication and trust with my man. I mean the tape really gave me something to aspire to. Thank you.

FROM: SEECEE@HOTMAIL.COM

TO: ALADY27@EARTHLINK.NET

SUBJECT: YOU

You can have that level of intimacy. But you're gonna have to be honest and ask for it. You get there by having no secrets. In fact I urge you to tell him about us. You open that door and I know you'll be surprised at what secrets of his will pop out.

FROM: ALADY27@EARTHLINK.NET

TO: SEECEE@HOTMAIL.COM

SUBJECT: NOT TIME

I believe in my heart you're right, but it's not time for that yet. You spend so much time letting a person know you, opening up to them and then, after all that time and commitment, you spring a whole new dimension of yourself on them. I guess I'm not sure how he'll react. I do want to be honest. Being honest is easier said (or not said) than done.

Chapter 15

This was it. Our first full-fledged fall into "sexual frankness." I stood in the wings, watching the stage, the monitor and, most important of all, our studio audience. Not only were my fingers and toes crossed but my stomach was twisted into a mammoth knot.

Circus Dix and Serena Sin sat on either side of Nick Shaw. I'd pre-interviewed each myself after Tanya and I sifted through a year of AVN's, the pornography industry's leading trade publication, a place to find the #1 DVDs, reviews of new product and full-color ads for movies never mentioned in *Variety*. The Professor had turned us on to the magazine, so that investment was already paying dividends.

Circus Dix was a tall, muscular but not particularly handsome brown man with, reputedly, the thickest penis in a business where size definitely mattered. Thankfully the bald, round-headed, smooth-faced Circus wore a tan, loose-fitting Armani knockoff that obscured his career-defining assets. His debate partner was not nearly as modest. Ms. Sin was a raven-haired half-Chinese, half-white lady in an incredibly low-cut light peach pastel dress with matching platform sandals and a gold anklet. Nick Shaw seemed delighted with the conversation, which, in our high-minded parlance, was an "exploration" of racism in porno.

"RIP, which stands for Racism in Porno," Circus explained, "was founded to highlight the prejudice against black men in the porn industry that keeps wages low and, forgive the phrase, Nick, but prevents us from becoming bigger attractions."

"Well," Nick wondered, "how does this prejudice manifest itself?"

"Quite simply," Circus replied, "black penises are considered too big, too long and too threatening." This elicited a murmur from our audience that wouldn't have impressed Springer, but was quite unusual in our house. My stomach tightened. Circus continued, "Serena here has told interviewers she won't work with brothers because they have penises down to our knees."

There was a palpable "Whoa" after that. I'd pre-interviewed Circus (aka Theo Morris) myself, so I knew he would have no trouble expressing himself, which is why we'd flown him in from Cali. But he was even more aggressive than I'd imagined.

Shaw had an amused look on his face—as if his life's ambition had always been to discuss genitalia on national television. "Well, Ms. Sin, what do you say to that?" he asked.

"Nick, that's such a simplification." Serena spoke in a light, Valley Girlish voice that belied her sultry appearance. Serena Sin (aka Patricia Chin) had graduated with a degree in economics from USC and had a very pragmatic view of life. "It's about economics, Nick. I'm under contract at Vivid Video and we aren't allowed to work with black guys because we can't sell the resulting film to Playboy and other cable erotic channels. It's the market that's driving these decisions, not the girls."

There was certainly titillation in this material, but Ms. Sin spoke so matter-of-factly that I didn't feel as embarrassed as when Circus spoke. I couldn't tell if that was simply due to the subject or because Circus was a black man playing the stud role with too much gusto.

"But," Circus came back saying, "when you let that happen, you play into a lot of racist stereotypes. You're biracial, so you know how hard it is."

"Look," she said, exasperated, "I just wanna make it clear, I love black men. But that's not the issue."

"But what about that statement, Ms. Sin?" Shaw said. "I understand you've made that comment about black men on a number of occasions."

"Listen," she began earnestly, "you gotta understand how insecure the world I work in is. Most of these tapes and DVDs are purchased by lonely white men who jerk off when their wife goes to get groceries. They equate sex with fast food. The last thing they want is to be distracted from their pleasure by seeing Circus' member in firing range of pale skin. So I say whatever I have to in order to make them comfortable."

"Ms. Sin, you have quite a way with words." It was Shaw, whose horns were showing. Flirting with a female journalist or actress had always been fine. But I wasn't sure how sucking up to a porno star would play. Ms. Sin, apparently quite used to men making fools of themselves in her presence, just ignored his leer and pressed her point. "Let me add this—I don't get on the cover of many magazines in my industry. Not like white women of my caliber. Nor do I get the same dollars for personal appearances, though I'm as much in demand as the other female performers out there. Everybody's interested in sex, Nick, but there are still barriers when it comes to people's fantasies, and I'm a victim as much as Circus."

"I agree with that," Circus interjected. "The truth is that sex is all fantasy. It's that space in your head where you dream of the things you'd like to do."

"But, Circus," Shaw said, "Ms. Sin is implying that there's no audience for the fantasy you provide, that we are as divided sexually as we are in other aspects of our national life." Gold star for Shaw there, managing to frame our dig into depravity as a meditation on the nation's soul. That's why he gets the big bucks.

Now Circus got quite heated. "No, Nick, that's not what's going on. The white men who control the porno biz don't reflect what's going on out there in the country. I believe America is interested in seeing all kinds of sex, all kinds of ways, by all kinds of people." This actually got applause from many in our audience. Could it be that this topic was actually working?

With a smirk, Shaw added, "As Prince said, 'Black, white, Puerto Rican, everybody just a-freakin'.'"

"That's right," Circus agreed. "Wouldn't it be fun to see me and Serena displaying our talents together?" Now Circus was going for his and the audience's temperature rose three degrees at least.

Luckily Shaw regained control as we headed into the home stretch. "I think the real question, Circus, is why should my viewers care? Is RIP about just getting a few well-endowed black men a little cash or is this about putting a spotlight on how racism can penetrate even a place as open-minded as the sex industry?"

"Well, Nick," Circus said, smiling, "when you put it like that, I'll have to say both."

"No equivocating there, huh?" Shaw replied. He'd pulled the segment back to dry land before we'd drowned in the muck. As slick as a PR man over an expensive lunch, he wrapped it all up. "You can reach RIP at www.ripitgood.com, while Serena Sin's latest Vivid video, *Dim Sum Sin*, is available at fine stores everywhere. Thanks for tuning in and always remember, 'The sun is always shining somewhere. Shouldn't it shine on you?'"

As our theme music, Billy Joel's "Pressure," came up and the credits rolled, I scanned our audience for signs of displeasure, discomfort and disgust. I spotted two deeply wrinkled brows and maybe a couple on the border of outrage. But they were well balanced by leers, smiles and a giddy sense that they'd watched something naughty well camouflaged.

Afterward Shaw, Walker from the syndicator, the other producers, Tanya and myself sat in the conference room and ran the numbers. In New York, where we ran live, we studied the phone calls, e-mails and instant ratings, and it was all overwhelmingly positive. The few people who hated this show broadcast really hated it. Some said they'd never watch us again. Others claimed porn industry racism was a "nonissue," that we'd exploited the topic solely for its T&A value. And, of course, they were right.

But the majority was as forgiving as the polls were to Clinton after Monica. Either they felt it was a legitimate issue or that they'd been informed about something they'd previously known nothing about. In both cases, voyeuristic viewers masked their enjoyment of our carefully presented cheap thrill. However you looked at it, the feedback was encouraging.

So much so that as the meeting was breaking up Shaw pulled me aside. "You know, Dean, Serena invited me to join her and a few friends for dinner. You wanna—pun definitely intended—come?"

"No, man. That's all yours."

"You sure? Your girl's not back yet, is she?"

"It doesn't matter, Shaw. What you're proposing doesn't sound sanitary."

"You would say that, Dean, you damn Dr. Spock. By the way, I understand that your able assistant is dining with Mr. Dix."

I looked over to where Tanya was gathering up her notes. "Isn't she the one who found him?"

"Kind of. The Professor turned us on to the AVN and she saw his RIP ad. She's found a great many guests for us these last two years."

"Yeah, yeah, yeah," Shaw replied dismissively. "But what I think is that there's more to your little Tanya 'than is written about in your philosophies, Horatio.'"

Tanya saw us gaze her way, smiled tightly and then headed out of the room as if she didn't wanna chat. "I don't know, Shaw," I said, my mind traveling over this new sexual terrain. "I'm feeling a little like Alice after she's fallen down the rabbit hole."

"Yeah," he said with an edge, "isn't it gonna be great seeing what's down there?"

* * *

About two A.M. my phone rang and a voice I needed to hear filled the receiver. "Wake up, sleepyhead." Millie spoke with a slight slur. "It's your future calling." There was a lot of background noise—classic rock music, plates being tapped by folks, the too loud arguments of people holding drinks.

"Where are you, Mill?"

"San Francisco."

"No. Not the city—the place. Sounds like a bar."

"Yes, it is." Then someone asked her a question—a man— that made her giggle.

"Mill?"

"Do you love me, Dean?"

"Of course."

She spoke to someone at the other end: "He says 'Of course.' And this ring shows he means it."

"MILLIE!"

"Yes, darling."

"Who are you talking to?"

"Oh, Jeff and Sal and Steve."

"And they are?"

"They run a fulfillment house out of Blair, Iowa."

"Blair, Iowa, huh. So why are you all in a bar in Frisco?"

"We're gonna invest in them—maybe." A male voice said something and Millie replied, "You wish."

"MILLIE," I said again with irritation.

"Yes, Dean. You love me, right?"

"Millie, you are drunk at a bar with three men I don't know in San Francisco. Unless they're gay, I'm not happy right now."

"You should be," she responded, sounding a little testy herself. "I called because they were teasing me. They said I've been away from home so long that, if they were you, they'd be out getting into trouble. Well, Dean, you showed them."

"Hurray for me, Millie."

"That's right, baby."

"Millie, when are you coming home?"

"Ah, Dean, I don't think I'll be able to come back for a few more weeks. Now that I'm on the road, the company wants me to visit some other businesses and see how they look on a day-to-day basis. I'm sorry."

"So am I. Do you love me?"

"More than ever, Dean."

"Good. Come home soon, Mill."

"I will, Dean. Do you love me?"

"More than ever."

"Now," she said softly, "I feel guilty, Dean." She must have walked into a hallway or the ladies' room because the background noise had faded. "I'm out here and you're back there asleep."

"Was asleep."

"Well, don't worry. I'm going to my hotel soon as we hang up."

"Well," I said glibly, "I'm hanging up now. Go to your room."

"Yes, Daddy Dean. I'm leaving right now. I love you."

"I love you too."

Afterward I lay looking up at the ceiling. It was great for her to call but it was bad what my imagination did with it. I saw her in bed with Jeff and Sal and Steve. I saw her on her cell calling me as all three men fondled her body and licked those luscious legs. I used these images to justify my actions with Bee. The real-world side of me knew better. These images I'd concocted had nothing to do with reality. Millie was just doing what all businesspeople do on the road—socialize, bullshit and bond. That's why you go out there. Building relationships is the entire gig.

But in that wonderfully self-rationalizing part of the male psyche, I needed to ease the guilt I had about Bee and me. Not even married and already in serious denial. I fell asleep with the feel of Bee's handcuffs around my wrists and her tongue inside my mouth.

Chapter 16

"B lood flow is the key to life," my father said as he cut into his piece of vegan fried chicken. "You know I've always said that. Stay limber, stay loose. Avoid stuff that clogs the heart, like that pork, that beef and all that slop black folks have been ingesting since we wore chains that weren't jewelry." He picked up a slice of his fake, wheat-gluten-disguised-as-poultry and stuffed it happily in his mouth. "It took me years to learn that, you know."

We were in Vegetarian Paradise 2, a vegan restaurant just off Sixth Avenue in Greenwich Village, and a must visit for Daddy when he made his annual pilgrimage north. VP2 was notable because its proprietor, an amiable man named Mr. Chung, concocted pseudo-meat and -fish dishes out of wheat gluten and soybean. At VP2 you could order pork chops, salmon steak and teriyaki chicken or, more accurately, a disgustingly healthy illusion of them. Here, your basic cardiovascular system–clogging American fare had been rehabilitated into organically safe health food. It looked real and sometimes, with the right sauce, even tasted real.

When I was a kid, Grandpa Chance dined just like every other black man of his generation—bacon, eggs, grits and coffee so thick it could pass for coal. When he withered away due to diabetes, my father responded to this painful wake-up call by re-evaluating everything that entered his mouth. One day he walked into our Lower East Side apartment with arms full of frozen health food from a store on Astor Place that served granola grocery shoppers. Momma was a woman who saved the grease from her fried fish in metal cans by the sink and sprinkled hot sauce on everything in the kitchen except our Raisin Bran. She saw Daddy's new culinary direction as an insult to her cooking and her waistline, which, admittedly, was expanding like crack did in the eighties. That fateful day was the beginning of the end of their marriage.

Maybe if Daddy had been less abrupt in his dietary change and more thoughtful in his explanation, the transition would have gone smoothly. Instead he came in the house with this strange-tasting "healthy" food and demanded that Momma's can of lard be disposed of as quickly as yesterday's horoscope. She drank sugar, sweet iced tea; he guzzled soy milk. She savored pork fried rice; he favored brown rice. She excelled at cooking anything made with processed flour; he came to desire all by-products of the mighty bean called soy.

My stomach became the battleground for this culinary war. For breakfast with Daddy, who drove me to school most mornings on his bus, it was granola, soy milk and fruit. Dinner with Momma, whose bus routes ended earlier than his, so she got home first, was candied yams, macaroni and cheese, and every part of the pig you could buy (and that's a lot of pig!). It got so I started avoiding meals with either of them, waking early and grabbing Egg McMuffins and staying out late playing basketball to escape pork.

Unfortunately for my family, but happily for my intestines, Daddy and Momma finally decided their culinary differences were unresolvable. Her menu was as old school as an Otis Redding ballad, while his dining habits were as progressive as Erykah Badu's head wrap. Momma moved back to the Tidewater area of her native Virginia and still drove school buses and ate all the pork she could get her lips around (and in Virginia that's a lot of pork). Pops relocated to the ATL (Atlanta to us outsiders) and married a macrobiotic H&R Block employee, who saw the mighty soybean as God's blessed handiwork.

"So," he said after greedily downing a glass of fresh squeezed carrot juice, "I see your show is getting a little spicier of late."

"Yeah," I admitted, "what do you think?"

"There's a place for talk of sexual congress in any intelligent discourse." My father had a high school education and a prep school vocabulary. Growing up, I remember him watching William Buckley's *Firing Line* with a dictionary and thesaurus by his knee. You never knew what Daddy would say when properly lubricated by vegetable juice. "Your man Nick Shaw handles it well. How you feel about your endeavor's new direction?"

"Well, I'm a little worried. We worked so hard to build a quality show, and this seems like an easy way to slide into Ricki Lake land."

"I understand you feeling that way. You've never been very comfortable dealing with sex, Dean."

"What makes you say that?"

"I tried to explain the ins and outs to you many times during your formative years, but you never wanted to engage in a dialogue."

"Daddy, what kid enjoys those heart-to-hearts with their parents?"

"True," he said with a wistful look. "Judging by your soiled bed sheets, you figured out the basics."

We both laughed at this one, especially when I added, "Yeah, it was the only time I wanted to clean anything in my room. I'd leave my socks dirty, and my T-shirts funky, but the night after I jerked off I'd be down in the laundry room with the bottle of Tide."

We laughed some more, sharing events unspoken of when I was a child, but now humorous to two grown men. However, my father wasn't gonna let a little thing like laughter lead him off point. "But I still meant what I just said, Dean. You were unusually shy when it came to copulation. I was an open book. You could have asked me anything but you never did." I was surprised at Daddy's tone—there was a hurt in his voice that was unexpected and, I felt, unwarranted.

I wasn't gonna tell him about my current love life with all the scandalous details. But his voice cut me a bit. After their divorce I'd lived with Momma and, as a result, was closer to her, which was a sore subject for him. So, after my daddy's admission and the strong, tart cup of wheatgrass, I spilled to him everything that had happened between my romantic weekend with Millie and my recent, perspiration-producing nights with Bee.

While I was talking, my father's face (which is basically my face, except that it was thinner with brighter, better beige skin) went through a remarkable transformation, from parental concern to quiet disapproval to shock to lechery without passing "Go!"

"Dean," he said when I'd finished, "that's a remarkable tale, one that makes me so happy for you."

"The whole thing?"

"Oh, yes. Think about this, son. You have a woman captivated by you and full of desire to be your wife. And in her you've finally found someone you feel strongly enough about to give a ring. I'm so happy about that, son."

"And that makes me happy, Daddy."

"Now you have this other woman, a completely different kind of woman, who sees you as a sexual being. Not a husband or a provider or any of that stable, build-a-nest thinking. She is excited by your presence."

"I guess."

"Well, what else do you want out of your time on earth, Dean? Most men get one or the other or none of the above. You are being admired by two women of different kinds for different things at the same time."

"I haven't seen it that way, Daddy."

"Well, you need to and you need to enjoy nirvana while you're there. It won't last. This Bee thing is temporary. A way to release a little pre-marriage anxiety. Don't sweat it and don't take it seriously. Just don't ever let Millie know. This episode is something you take to your grave. I mean, the closest I ever came to something like that was one night with your mother and Nancy Auerbach—"

"Who?"

"A Catholic school driver we met. One night we all got drunk together after work. That was something."

"Daddy, what are you saying?"

"Oh, this was before you were born, son." He got that wistful look again and that pulled himself back into the now. "Anyway, my point is don't do your normal Virgo fretting, Dean. Just enjoy this moment for what it is. The past is done. The future is always unexpected. Right now is what you're living for." He reached in his pocket and handed me some pills.

"What's this do, Daddy?"

"Yohimbe. It's a natural potency pill. Ingest as much of that as possible, call up that Bee woman and then e-mail me the outcome."

"What's this do?"

"Everything a man like you needs."

"Daddy."

"Don't thank me yet, Dean. Just let your blood flow, son. Let it flow."

Chapter 17

The net is supposed to be the information superhighway. We just ride onto the on ramp and roll swiftly to enlight-enment. But to me it is a collection of press releases, unverified gossip and colorful, cluttered graphic-filled pages that take up lots of everyone's time. It can be a frustrating place to drive across, particularly when you don't know the right exit.

At MTV.com she was simply B. Cole, maker of videos for R. Kelly, Ginuwine, D'Angelo and other black singers who disliked shirts. I noticed all the videos listed under her name were for male singers. Vibe.com was somewhat more informative. In a "Next" section profile there was a lovely close-up of her face and that chilly smile to accompany a text that mentioned B. Cole Productions, her various male-oriented videos and that she'd attended Brooklyn's Pratt Institute. In the BK she'd fallen in with a crew of poets who gigged at slams around the Apple. The legend goes that Bee picked up a video camera and began creating sexy, innovative tapes of her poetry posse that were sold at their performances.

Some Def Jam staffer saw the flicks, offered her a real video and biz started to boom. "I bring a sensuality to music video that no man can match," she bragged in *Vibe*. The rest of the piece was fluff—her favorite food was Indian, her designer Prada. No mention of anything else useful.

Her production company was based in Silicon Alley on Broadway in the Twenties, according to the B. Cole Productions Web site. A call revealed it was manned by a nineteen-year-old intern with piss-poor communication skills ("Yo, son, B. Cole Productions? Get at me"), who revealed, in a rather haphazard, ass backward way, that Bee rarely came in, communicating with her office and clients only via e-mail and cell phone. The work was contracted out to a regular crew who was mostly black and primarily female. "Could I have her e-mail address?" I asked and the intern said, "B.Cole@ B.Cole.com, son. There you go." Click.

B.Cole.com was her official Web site, a place where you could watch clips of her videos or submit budgets, treatments, etc., and otherwise engage in a bit of e-commerce. It was not, however, a place where I could safely inquire into the real-life desires of my enigmatic playmate.

Tanya called around to the record companies under the guise of researching Bee as a guest, and all she came back with were glowing reviews and a hint—just a whisper really—of gossip. "She really gets into the heads of the men she does videos for," she was told mysteriously by one executive. A nice start. Still, Tanya didn't know I wanted real dirt but I was too nervous to push her about finding it. Instead I had Tanya bring Bee up with Mr. Sex, Professor Lawson, but the feedback was unilluminating. "Her work is provocative within a commercial medium," Lawson told her. Fine for a paper, but of no use to me.

Anyone as freaky as Bee had to have built a rep in somebody's circle. Unfortunately I wasn't plugged into the world of black pop music. If Bee had worked with Wynton or Marcus Roberts or even Harry Connick Jr., I'd have a way in. But I had no access to the world of ghetto glamour that Bee obviously resided in. After a day of phone calls, Tanya, quite naturally, inquired, "Are we gonna book her for a show, Dean?" I just shook my head. "No, Tanya," I answered with the straightest of faces. "Miss Bee Cole doesn't seem quite provocative enough for *The Nick Shaw Show*."

Chapter 18

The next few days I felt like I was drifting back to normalcy. No calls from Bee. We'd taped a couple of shows that were straight and smart, just like we used to. It didn't mean I wasn't still troubled by all the changes in my world, but things didn't seem either as overwhelming or strange. It was a Wednesday and, as I had for years, I used that night for lifting. I got out my weights and my workout bench and began pumping hard. I needed some pressure released and lifting always did that for me. I'd rather my muscles hurt than my brain. James Carter's mid-nineties classic *The Real Quietstorm* played low in the background, giving me a sonic massage even as my muscles bunched together.

After I lifted I sat on my bench and looked at the apartment, taking inventory of my life. I lived in a pricey, old prewar building in the East Twenties off Park with a doorman, laundry room and fake Art Deco fixtures. It all could have looked elegant. Some of my neighbors' apartments did. Unfortunately my decor was vintage college dorm, not swinging singleton. I wasn't much of a ladies' man—I mostly liked working, watching the Knicks and having a faithful girl-friend—and in that order.

Now I was on a new path and I didn't know where it was leading. The sex was dope. But what of Millie and marriage? Could our years of love be so easily erased by a few weeks of amazing poontang? My life—personal and professional—felt like it was being rewritten by Danielle Steele. I was mulling this and doing stomach crunches when the phone rang. When I said, "Hello," the voice on the other end snickered.

"Oh," Bee said, "you're out of breath. Thinking of me?"

"Not at this minute. But it could change."

"It will."

There was a knock at my door. I walked over and through the peephole saw a woman's puckered red lips. A moment later Bee was in my apartment looking stylish but much more midday professional than I'd seen to date. "Just in the neighborhood," she told me as she looked around my place with an appraising eye.

"How'd you get in the building?"

"It's surprising how sweet doormen can be." Bee's eye found a picture of Millie and me. She picked it up, smiled cryptically and said, "You two make a very sensible looking couple."

Fuck you is what I thought as I took the photo from her hands. What I said was "Thanks" and placed it back on a table. "Don't you think you should have called first before stopping over?" My tone was scolding. This was my place—my turf. I wasn't gonna let her play with me in my house. "If I did this to you, you'd be freaking out."

She sat down on my workbench and looked up at me.

"That's the difference between us, Dean. I'm the type of person who pushes things and you're always a little afraid to test the boundaries. Well, I have a treatment for that." She pulled two legal pads out of her leather briefcase, put them in her lap and then patted the spot next to her on the workout bench, suggesting I sit down.

"Dean," she said reasonably, "I want you to write down your sexual fantasies on this pad and I'll write down mine, too. When we're done we'll each pick one of the other's fantasies to fulfill. How's that sound to you?"

I sat next to her and inhaled some wonderful perfume, feeling the sweat on my body dry to sand. "It sounds," I replied evenly, "kinda dangerous."

"Good," she said, "so let's get to writing."

Immediately Bee began scribbling on one notepad in tight, black letters. I took the other pad and wrote slowly, as if I was squeezing out ideas one drop at a time. Just when I was getting going, Bee ripped off the top sheet of her pad, a sign of creative superiority that sapped the gusto right out me. So I put my pen down and read her small, precise writing on the ripped-out sheet. "Damn," I said. But Bee was oblivious. She just kept on writing.

Time passed. I actually had down two, maybe three, good ideas and then—rip!—there went another very full yellow sheet of paper. Feeling impotent once more, I stopped and read her latest salvo. I'd read half the page when I just said, "That's it. That's it, Bee."

"Huh?"

"This is too much, okay? Let's just read what we have, alright?"

"Okay," she said, disappointed. "If you wanna go with what you have, fine. Let me look."

I handed her my one sheet and then found myself curled up on my bench like a cat. Glancing at my meager output, Bee cracked, "Prolific, huh?" and chuckled. At that instant I knew this was without doubt the most embarrassing moment of my life. "Godiva chocolates, huh? That's pretty basic."

"I've had no complaints."

"Well, consider the source, Dean." Then her insolence ceased, her eyes got wide and her red mouth opened a bit. "Oh, Dean, looks like we have a winner. And it's so personal. Let's make number three happen."

"You sure? I mean it's kind of ill."

"That's why I like it. So now pick one of mine."

"Where do I start?"

"Good point," she agreed. She took the pages from my hand and scanned them. "Why not this one at the top of page two? It's relatively simple, I think."

I read it and, compared to her other ideas, it seemed fun and within my means. But it did have one difficulty. "We'll need help, you know?"

"Don't worry," she answered, "I have just the person."

"So I'm gonna meet one of your friends."

This idea, like much I seemed to do, amused her greatly. "I don't know if that's the word I'd use," she said coyly, "but sure, 'friend' is as good a word as any."

FROM: SEECEE@HOTMAIL.COM

TO: ALADY27@EARTHLINK.NET

SUBJECT: A PROBLEM

We have to break off communication for a few weeks. Something's come up in my life. Something I have to deal with, that I have to get out of my life, one way or the other. Can't be disturbed right now—and you disturb me. I'll reach out to you in a few weeks.

FROM: ALADY27@EARTHLINK.NET

TO: SEECEE@HOTMAIL.COM

SUBJECT: YOUR PROBLEM

I hope it's not too serious, though it does sound like real trouble. But actually the timing is good for me. It's time to get settled again. Time to re-establish the ties that can always be strengthened. So take your time and be good to yourself. You are so analytical, maybe it's time to make moves from your heart. Of course, that advice may not be helpful, but I feel a need for you to cut loose. Maybe that makes sense. I hope it does.

Chapter 19

It took me about a week to find the appropriate hotel. Tanya thought she was researching a possible segment when, in truth, my assistant was facilitating Bee's fantasy life. The spot she found—dark, slightly moldy and thankfully discreet—was way up on the West Side, right around the corner from Columbia. They didn't mind when I brought in the 78 player and my own bed sheets. I arrived at room 33 first, setting up the vintage record player, putting on the gold-colored sheets Bee had requested and burning the sweet honey incense I'd purchased for the occasion.

I was there for a half-hour waiting when Pamlesha arrived. I knew she was coming, but seeing her in the flesh was still a shock. This was the girl I saw that day on Central Park West. This was the woman dancing on the video screen in the Virgin Megastore. At five-foot-ten, with burnt orange skin and blond hair, Pamlesha was quite a sight. She was also, at least as far as I could tell, a gorgeous sphinx. For all her beguiling beauty, I found Pamlesha a guarded, highly unapproachable presence. When I'd opened the door, she greeted me with a polite "Nice to meet you," and her name. Other than that, conversation had been slight and superficial. Her vibe made it clear she was here to please Bee and Bee alone. I was only a potentially useful nuisance. Being a man would in no way make me the evening's center of attention.

At 7:15, I placed the heavy 78 rpm record on the player and the melancholy voice of Bessie Smith sang "The St. Louis Blues," a dark, sexy song of longing that I thought appropriate for what Bee intended. Right on time at 7:17, there was a knock on the unlocked door and Bee, in a sheer black dress and black mules, walked in. She closed the door behind her, smiled and then slid that black dress off her shoulders and onto the floor, revealing the taut reddish brown skin that had led me so astray. With a soft sashay Bee moved over to the bed and lay down upon it with her mules still on.

"Open the bottles," she told us, "and pour the champagne over me."

We uncorked our bottles of Dom P and, slowly and meticulously, poured the contents across her body, making her nipples harden, filling the space at her navel and turning her skin a shiny gold. Pamlesha went right for it. Down on her knees, hands behind her back, Pamlesha began drinking champagne out of the folds and surfaces of Bee's upper body.

"Dean," Bee said hoarsely, "lick the champagne off my feet."

Like a good soldier, I moved to the foot of the bed, removed the mules and then drowned Bee's feet in the last of my Dom P. Bee was moaning low now. She got a little louder when I took her toes into my mouth, first sucking them individually and then taking in as many as I could at one time.

I don't know how long I was down there or Pamlesha was

up there, but by the time we met in the middle of Bee's body we were both tipsy and our jaws were tired. Yet we didn't let that stop us. We kept pleasing Bee until our faces met mid-stomach. Pamlesha took my face in her hands and then kissed me. Bee sat up now and cradled both our heads, manipulating our movements as we tongued each other. Then Bee spread her legs and pushed us slowly down toward her groin.

"Each of you take a hole."

Bee was the conductor and, acting as her instruments, we played the notes she wanted to hear for the rest of the night.

Two days later Bee was conductor again, orchestrating my strange and special composition. Round midnight, Evander drove us to "Alphabet City," the series of thoroughfares in the East Village named after the first four letters of the alphabet, a part of town I knew well and had mostly tried to forget, though this warm evening was all about righting just a bit of that past. Bee sat up under me, but I was not comfortable.

"You don't have to do this for me."

"I owe it to you, Dean," she said. "Besides, I'm looking forward to this."

"That girl from the other night, Pamlesha, looked very familiar. She didn't say much, but I guess she didn't have to."

Bee just stared out the window. "You probably conjured her up from one of your dreams, Dean," she replied slyly.

"Yeah, right out of your telephone book."

I could feel Bee didn't wanna discuss our sexual aide—just as Pamlesha had been as tight-lipped as an attorney. Once Bee showed up, of course, those lips had parted. After it was over, and I'd fallen asleep on the champagne-dampened sheets, Pamlesha had disappeared back into Bee's notebook, soon to reappear no doubt in some crooner's next video.

Changing the subject, Bee asked, "So are we almost there?"

I looked out the window and nodded my head. "It's on the left. Three fifteen," I answered. A public housing project, a place where the poor are stacked up like inventory in some dingy back room. Much of my young life had been spent inside this very stack of boxes, but I hadn't been back in years.

"Bee, this might be dangerous," I said as we stood on the sidewalk.

"That's why I'm here, Dean."

"Maybe Evander should come along."

"No, he'll stay in the car. Besides, he might get nosy and watch." Evander stood on the other side of the car and, as usual, said nothing. I glanced over at Evander, whose eyes surveyed the streets, looking aware and quite formidable. He'd be fine. But where we were going, we could have used some backup.

The lobby, to my surprise, was empty. What was predictable were the grime, the candy wrappers and the flood of memories. You could hear the low rumble of life pulsating through the walls. There was a long row of metal mailboxes along one wall. I walked over to one and tapped it.

"This used to be our mailbox."

"Belongs to the Santiagos now."

"Guess that's right," I replied quietly.

"Still haunted, Dean?"

Trying to sound sage, I observed, "Where you grow up always follows you, no matter how far you go."

Bee took my arm and said, "How's about we exorcise the evil spirits?" She guided me over to the elevator bank, pushed a button and then took my hand, squeezing it hard. When the doors opened, like a dog leading the blind, she took me onboard. Bee rubbed her nose at the rank aroma—a blend of piss and industrial-strength cleanser—and pressed the sixteenth-floor button.

"Never got any when you lived here?"

"I was a kid, Bee."

"That didn't stop your neighbors, did it?"

On the eighth floor the door opened and an attractive teenaged girl got on and gave us the once-over. We'd gone up three floors when the girl asked, "You looking for Z?"

"No," I said firmly.

Ignoring me, she continued, "He's on fourteen. Fourteen C."

"Thanks, hon," Bee said too sweetly. Then, with a giggle, "Maybe on the way down."

At the fourteenth floor, the young lady exited. She turned just as the door began to close and looked hard at Bee, like she was trying to place her.

"I guess we look like tourists trying to cop," I observed. To which Bee replied, "We kind of are, aren't we?"

It occurred to me that our teenaged friend might tell Z or some of Z's friends about our presence and, for any number of nefarious reasons, they could come looking for us. That increased my nervousness, but I didn't share my concerns with Bee. The elevator door opened and the sixteenth floor was just as I remembered—unwashed, dusty tiled floors and harsh metallic light. I squeezed her hand and we turned left.

"This way."

I led Bee into the stairway, where the light was even harsher than in the hallway. But vision didn't matter. I was moving on memory. I stepped on an empty Trojan package as I put my shoulder to a door labeled ROOF. It opened easily.

Back out in the New York night. To our right was the Williamsburg Bridge, old and cranky; to our left, as vibrant as Christmas lights, were the towers of midtown. I suddenly felt very frustrated. I hadn't really traveled that far. I lived uptown but I was a brief ride from this old roof and all the inadequacy it recalled. Was I confronting my fear or indulging it?

I turned around and Bee opened her blouse to reveal a scarlet bra that blazed through the roof's murky lights. I walked forward as Bee stepped back toward the roof's edge.

"All these years," she said, "you've wanted to have a girl up on this roof—just like all the cool guys, just like everyone but you. And now you have me, Dean. Come on."

I moved toward Bee until her back was against the roof's edge. I dropped my pants. I dropped my shorts. I ripped off her scarlet panties. I grabbed her ass. I slipped on the condom that suddenly dangled from Bee's lips.

Bee leaned back. Her torso fell back over the building's edge, supported only by my hands. I entered her. Bee let her hands fall free so that they dangled as we made love. My back strained and shuddered under the effort of fucking and holding her, but I didn't stop, couldn't stop, this dangerous dance. I knew if I weakened Bee could fall and so might I. I could feel God's eyes on my back as he looked down on us two sinners and laughed at the judgment he had in store.

"Oh, shit!" A girl's voice behind us. Not too close. Watching. Surprised. Fascinated. Bee ordered me, "Don't stop!

Don't stop!" and I didn't. Bee grabbed me by the neck and intensified her movements. I came with a shudder and collapsed like a demolished building.

As I gathered myself and my clothes, Bee walked over to our witness—that teenaged girl. Bee said, "You recognize me, don't you?"

"Yeah," the girl said. "I saw you on 'Making of a Video.'"

"Aside from letting you watch us fuck, can I do anything else for you?"

Unfazed by Bee's bluntness, the girl replied, "Well, my name is Syndee. I'm a singer and I have this demo tape."

"Well, Syndee, give it up, then."

Syndee handed it over as Bee stared into her eyes. Now Syndee's cool was wilting a bit. She said, "My number's on it," rather unsteadily.

"I'll listen. If I like it I'll call." Then, enjoying Syndee's discomfort, Bee added, "Who knows, I may call anyway."

"Okay," Syndee said. "Well, you have a good evening." Then she peered over at me as I pulled up my pants. "You too." I didn't say anything. I just pulled up my pants and felt a little dizzy as the blood rushed back to my brain. As Syndee left, Bee slipped the cassette into her bra.

"I'm ready to go, Dean," she said off-handedly. "What about you?"

In the elevator down, I felt extremely vulnerable and quite tired. I'd finally gone through a rite of passage that I'd missed years ago. But it felt more like exercise than nirvana. I had expected to feel cleansed somehow, that the enactment of this long-held fantasy would somehow erase my childhood pain. Instead it had just been exhausting, weird sex. Nothing more.

It struck me that I'd gone as far with Bee as I could or even really cared to. With our list of fantasies we were now manufacturing desire and that, finally, wasn't enough. By robbing this fantasy of its mystique by consummating it, we had succeeded in putting an end to Bee's power over me. For the first time since we'd met I felt free. All I desired now was a shower and a slow, deep back rub.

Outside 315, an ambulance and two patrol cars stood, lights on, jammed up around Bee's car. There was glass everywhere from the car's smashed windows. Some blood was pooled along the sidewalk. "Oh my God!" said Bee, distant no longer. "Where's Evander!"

Chapter 20

The walls were a shade of institutional green I hadn't seen since elementary school. There was no swinging over-head light, so I squinted under the glare of my own embarrassment. Detective Toro sat across from me with a file. Every now and then he rubbed his protruding belly like my story was a particularly full meal.

"So," Toro said evenly, "let me get this straight. You went with Bee, whose last name you don't know, to visit your old neighborhood. You two lovebirds, who know virtually nothing about each other, then went stargazing on the roof. When you were through studying the moon over Manhattan you came downstairs to discover her car damaged and her driver beaten?"

"That's right, Detective."

"That's a strange story, Mr. TV Producer."

"One thing my job has taught me," I countered, "is that the truth is often strange."

"And one thing this job has taught me is that bullshit stinks." This was Detective Anderson, a tall, smoldering black man who seemed to enjoy standing over me like a high school bully preparing to steal my bus pass. "You know your girl-friend has no ID on her? But if you were some uptown lady going to cop in the projects for a sick thrill, I'd sure leave my ID home too."

"We did not go there to buy drugs, Detective."

"Then," Detective Toro inquired in his very reasonable voice, "what were you doing at 315 Avenue C, Mr. Chance, a notorious drug spot, in the middle of the night?"

"Look, Detectives, you can fish all you want, but we bought no drugs. You know that. I know that."

"Listen, Mr. Chance," Detective Anderson began roughly, "this is what I know: Your girl there seems to know a lot more about what's going on than you do. You have to ask yourself a question: Is that healthy for me?"

"What are you talking about?"

Detective Toro answered. "Mr. Chance, it's been a plea-sure meeting you, but it is not our job to straighten out your sex life."

Suddenly congenial, Detective Anderson added, "And give my regards to Nick Shaw. Nice show. A little dull, but it has integrity."

Outside the precinct, it felt like the temperature had risen ten degrees. Had a heat wave arrived while I sat inside? Or had roof fucking, no shower and police ridicule just plain overwhelmed my deodorant? Either way there was no Bee, no Evander. Just another humid New York night—one that had started and stayed weird. I walked, my eyes searching the street for a cab.

I pulled out my cell and punched in Bee's number. A com-puter voice informed me: "The cellular customer you have dialed is no longer with this service. This number is being re-assigned. Thank you."

She'd changed her number that quickly? Damn. Then, on cue, my cell rang. "Is that you?" I said excitedly.

"Of course it's me," Millie said. "Out of sight, out of mind, huh?"

"No, baby. It's so good to hear from you." I was gushing like a fire hose. "I miss you. I've missed you so much."

"That's good to know, Dean. And said so enthusiastically."

Sounding way too defensive, I asked, "How else would I say it?"

"Where are you? I tried you at home and at the job." My guilty anxiousness must have made her suspicious.

"I just took a walk, Millie. It's a pretty night. The first really hot night of the year."

I noticed a car, moving slowly, moving parallel to me.

"That's good, 'cause I'm coming in tomorrow afternoon. We wrapped things up in Silicon Valley earlier than I expected. Besides, we *do* have a wedding to plan."

"That's right, Mill." At that moment, after the events of this night, the idea of my marriage made me incredibly happy.

"So I'll see you tomorrow at the airport. I'm landing at JFK at four-thirty on American from San Francisco."

"I'll be there," I said. "I love you, Millie."

"Love you too. See you tomorrow."

I clicked off and then, like I'd gotten stabbed in the back, that chill ran up my spine. I spun around and saw that car was still clocking me, still moving strangely slow. The car had tinted windows but I could feel eyes boring into me. I made a move toward it and the car sped off.

Chapter 21

———————————————

Usually our weekly ideas meeting focused on newsmakers, business leaders and the odd starlet. This meeting was proceeding very professionally, as if sex had not become a recent concern of the show. No strippers. No porn stars. Nothing like that.

Then, suddenly, my recent sexual (mis)adventures seeped into my job. I started daydreaming about Pamlesha. I saw the woman kissing her on Central Park West. I saw her sucking on Bee's pedicured toes in a West Side hotel. I felt myself grabbing and sucking Pamlesha's nipples with Bessie Smith filling my ears. I guess that's why, right in the middle of our discussion of how to deal with the spread of AIDS among black and Hispanic youth, I suggested a show on the impact of music videos on teenage sexuality.

Ten minutes later, my thoughts had degenerated into pushing a segment on "the women of music video." Nick smiled happily at the idea; though we kept the discussion highbrow, beneath it was the latent Jenny Jones in all of us.

In the hallway after the meeting Nick put his arm around my shoulders and whispered, "Great idea, Dean. Wish I'd thought of it. T&A for a day. We can even have a live performance and the video girls can do their bit. I think that'll address the network's concerns."

"Thanks," I said, trying to hide my disappointment with my actions. Clearly Bee's influence on me had not gone away.

"You know," he said conspiratorially. "I've always thought you were an incredibly capable but incredibly straight guy. But Dean, you've blossomed."

Out of the corner of my eye, I saw Tanya listening with eyes full of disapproval.

"No, I'm the same guy," I told him. Though I had to admit, "Perhaps just a little more open."

"Whatever the reason, Dean, I think it's good for me and the show. Set this up as soon as possible."

Nick Shaw gave my arm a hearty squeeze and then headed off toward his office. Tanya came up beside me.

"Well, I heard what we're doing."

"Don't sound so disapproving. You helped inspire it."

"I took you to the Virgin Megastore," she countered, "that's all. It's one thing to look at sexual dysfunction and frustration in society. It's another just to let some airhead dancers talk."

"What," I said, offended. "You think I'm gonna let the show get tawdry?"

By now we were back in my office, where I immediately began writing the words "Video Dancers" on an index card.

"My father told me once you get turned out, it's hard to go back."

"Your daddy was a very smart man, Tanya. But, luckily for you, I am not your daddy. Here's what I want you to do—go find some expert on sexuality and music, someone's who's done a book or paper on the relationship between images and sex. A professor type."

"You mean like Professor Lawson?"

"God forbid, but you're right. It may finally be time to unleash the good professor on America. Also see if you can find a strong woman guest. Someone with that post-feminist, I-control-my-sexuality rap. How's that, Tanya? Sound like a Nick Shaw show now?"

Her attitude adjusted, Tanya replied brightly, "This is great, Dean. I'll get right on it." The young lady left my office with renewed enthusiasm for the show and, hopefully, me. I posted my "Video Dancers" card and studied my board. In between Toni Morrison hawking her latest opus and John McCain talking military preparedness, this segment sure stuck out. Made me contemplate my state of mind.

Millie would be arriving in a few hours and I wondered who would meet her. The man she'd agreed to marry just weeks ago? Or the freak I'd become? Or some new combination of both? In light of the topic I'd just pitched, I switched my television from CNN to BET. What filled the screen made my mouth drop open. A woman lay prone on a brass bed wearing a sheer black dress as a nasty R&B song wailed on. Two people—a man and a woman—appeared on either side of the bed holding champagne bottles. Not only did they pour the contents of those bottles on the woman's body, but the female doing the pouring was that ubiquitous beauty Pamlesha.

The video was like a postcard from a strange vacation, one

I needed to tear up and forget about. I clicked off the TV and, symbolically at least, tried to rip all those funky memories from my mind. Definitely time to go get my future bride.

I stood at the gate and took it all in. Businessmen in suits. Couples coming home from vacation. Children tugging on parents, parents dragging along kids. Folks dressed for the summer in T-shirts and linen. And Millie, with a computer bag slung over her shoulder and rolling a travel bag behind her, stopped when she saw me and said, "I don't believe you!" Then rushed toward me, like a kid just back from her first day at school. I guess it must have been the big sign I held up that in bright red letters read "Welcome Home Future Wifey."

"When d'you get so crazy?" she asked.

"I guess while I was waiting for you," I answered and then wrapped my arms, and the sign, around her waist and pulled her close to me. Relieved and happy, I vowed to pour my guilt (which was considerable) into treating this woman better than I ever had before.

Chapter 22

There is nothing better than being a man in the back of a yoga class. Most classes are filled with limber, lean women in skintight athletic wear, their legs and waist firmed by upward and downward dogs, various warrior poses, handstands and absolutely wonderful splits. From the back of the room a man—someone like me, for instance—surveys these pliant bodies and can be positively inspired by the mathematical and anatomic possibilities laid out before him.

Best of all is the sight of your own woman pushing her firm, tight ass up in the air in the downward dog yoga position. Not only does her ass aim toward the sky, but her head dangles between her legs in a wondrous approximation of doggie style that she seemingly can hold for hours. It is foreplay of the highest order. For the rest of the summer I joined Millie in exploring the positive effects of yoga practice for a happily monogamous couple. We'd bend our bodies together in class and then later savor the benefits of all that added flexibility in every part of our apartments.

All through *The Nick Shaw Show*'s midsummer hiatus, Bee didn't call and I felt no chills at night. I kept my television on

CNN and ESPN. I listened to Roy Hargrove, James Carter and some vintage Lee Morgan. When the office re-opened in August, Tanya handled the details of the music video segment, so I could keep my distance. I put my free time into following Millie around like a lovesick puppy. I followed her to yoga class, of course, and to various bridal shops, churches and florists.

Being with Millie was a relief, a return, a revelation. Millie wasn't gonna get me interrogated by the police or get me followed by some sicko ex. No, with Millie I knew what I was getting—comfort and back rubs and, not too far down the road, a home, something I really haven't had since my parents split up.

But then, to be truthful, the impact of Bee on my life didn't end just like that. There were reverberations. One day I closed my door and told Tanya to hold my calls. Said I had to do some reading. Then I called Millie. It was 3:30 in the afternoon.

When she came on the phone I asked, "Are you horny?"

"Dean, I am at work."

"Does that mean you wouldn't wanna fuck me if you could? I mean, jump on your desk and do me right now?"

"Dean, what's going on? You never used to talk to me this way before." She sounded delighted and surprised.

"Come on, Mill. No need to act shy now, baby. Talk to me."

A pause and then she inquired, "What are you doing right now?"

"I'm talking to you and touching my dick." Which is exactly what I was doing.

"Whoa."

"Whoa, indeed. Now"—my voice lowered and got more authoritative—"I want you to help me. Say my name, Millie."

"Dean."

"No, Millie," I ordered. "Say it soft. Say it how you say it when I'm in your bed and you like what I'm doing. I wanna hear it that way. You know how, Millie."

"Deannne." She stretched out my name until Dean had two syllables.

"Millie," I replied, "I love your pussy. It's so soft and wet and deep. Every time I'm with you I get lost in there. I never wanna leave. You know that, Millie." I could hear her breathing grow labored. She still repeated my name, saying it the way I like it. I could tell she was touching herself too.

"Are you touching yourself?" I ask.

"I can't do this."

"Just say my name and I'll say yours." My voice got hoarse and insistent. "Take your time, Millie. Take your time. We have all day and all damn night. Millie. Millie. Millie, my sweet, sweet lover."

I don't know who came first but we both did with low voices, sighs and the rubbing of fabric. Loved the sweet murmur of her voice in my ear. It was like her tongue had replaced my receiver. I felt her biting my lobe. And then there was silence. Finally Millie said, "Look what you made me do."

"No," I countered, "look what you made *me* do. The bottom of my desk is a mess."

"Well, I can't help you there," she said, "but I can clean you off. I'll wash you, baby. I'll be over to wash it tonight."

"Only after you make me wet again."

"Do I have to do that?" she asked impishly.

"You must," I ordered.

"Then I must. Bye," she said and then Millie hung up the phone.

The strange thing wasn't that I'd masturbated in my office, though that would fall under the heading of highly unusual. But the thing that was, well, scary or ironic or plain old strange (take your pick) was that some of my stuff fell onto the small corkboard tablet underneath my desk that was a mini-version of the big one on my wall. Since we'd started doing more and more risqué programs, too many staffers found it entertaining to come by and read my board, bemoaning the show's current direction, even as they poured over the cards with microscopic fascination. Now that board was dressed with my stuff. It made me laugh. I guess it landed where it belonged.

Chapter 23

M y fortieth birthday coincided with Labor Day and, to celebrate, Millie and I got a place out in Montauk, on the tip of Long Island beyond the Hamptons. That morning we rose at dawn and went fishing on a rented boat with Captain Singer and his handy mate Jimmy. Millie had never been on the ocean before, but she turned out to be a fine fisherwoman, reeling in a thirty-three-pound striped bass after a half-hour battle. Back on land, Jimmy cleaned and cut up our catch and then we stopped by Wok & Roll, a Chinese restaurant on Montauk Highway, where they fried and fricasseed our feast. Along with fried rice, broccoli and spring rolls, Millie and I devoured our catch and vowed to rent a house there next summer.

That night she gave me a bubble bath and then a long, loving massage with this oil she'd ordered from Paris. Against her wishes, I massaged her fishing-sore shoulders, so that we both smelled as sensual as a Left Bank mistress. If marriage was this good, why would anyone get divorced?

Around two in the morning I rolled over and felt a real chill. I pulled the blanket tight around me, but it wasn't the weather—it was that ill feeling I'd sometimes had with Bee. I opened my eyes and saw Millie staring at me.

In my worst Robert De Niro accent, I said, "You looking for me? Nobody here but me, baby."

"Dean, there's something I need to tell you. You are going to be my husband and I don't want there to be any secrets between us." My baby looked as nervous as I'd ever seen her. Her hands shook a bit, her voice wavered and she looked everywhere but my eyes.

"I agree. But know, whatever it is, it won't affect how I feel about you. And you don't have to tell me either. Just do what makes you comfortable, okay?"

There was a long pause and then Millie said in a weird voice, "I practice what some people might describe as a form of cybersex, though technically speaking, it isn't."

"Millie, what are you talking about?"

She reached over to her nightstand and placed her black Apple laptop onto the bed. She punched keys. A couple of minutes later I was reading an e-mail she'd sent to someone named SeeCee that closed with the lines, "I can't wait to see what bit of erotica you'll send on next. You know how much I enjoy you, us and the pictures I send you."

"What the fuck?" was my reaction.

"I'm sorry, Dean," she said, breaking into a sob. "I'm so sorry."

"How long have you been doing this?"

"Awhile," she said quite evasively.

"This looks like cybersex to me."

"Well," she began in a nervous tone, "cybersex is really real-time communication between two people talking back and forth in a dialogue. What I do isn't that, so it isn't really cybersex. Mostly what happens is that SeeCee sends me images. I tell him later how they made me feel. It's like an exchange of ideas in a way. He likes to hear what I think; I like to watch what he shows me." In a self-justifying aside Millie added, "So it's not the sleazy kind of cybersex you hear about."

I had to laugh at that. "All that rhetoric is fine. It's also bull-shit. You're communicating with some man about sex using the damn Internet. However you wanna define it, that shit is sexual."

"Yes, it is," she admitted.

"And you enjoy it?"

She simply said, "Yes," and that one word was so elo-quent—it communicated guilt, remorse and fear. I didn't know quite how to respond. I had no statement to make. I was pissed, definitely. But I was equally curious and that's what allowed me to keep my emotions in check. "So how come you didn't do it with me?"

In a pleading voice Millie explained herself: "You're real, Dean. Flesh and blood. I could have you anytime I wanted. This relationship—"

"Relationship? Is that what you call it?"

"I guess."

"Damn, Millie."

"It's all about fantasy, Dean. This is a person I could play with but never have to meet. And I never have met him. Never even been tempted. It was all in my mind, Dean. You must believe me."

Well, fuck me. There was more to her than I'd known in the years we'd been together. It was freaky and unexpected.

And somewhere in the dark, lusty part of my soul I was pleased. This revelation opened up—how can I put it?—"possibilities" for our marriage I never had considered before. I knew something deep and submerged about Millie and it tickled me.

Still, I thought it unwise to act enthusiastic. So in a stern but understanding voice I said, "It's cool, Millie. I believe you and I love you. Let's let the past stay in the past."

"You are so understanding."

We cuddled on the bed. I felt very magnanimous and good-hearted. What a good man I was.

"Dean," she said.

"Yeah, baby?"

"Do you have anything to tell me, Dean? Anything like this you wanna tell me about?"

I could feel her body tense as she waited anxiously for my reply. She was both afraid and hopeful. Not wanting to hear something that would really disturb her, but prepared nevertheless. Here is when I could have removed my big, stinky slime-covered skeleton stuck deep in my closet. Put it all away. Perhaps not tell the whole truth but enough that I wouldn't have to fear any later revelations. I could bury Bee with a few well-chosen words. Wouldn't that be cleansing?

"Yeah, baby, I do have something to admit," I began. "Every now and then I've flirted with my assistant, Tanya."

That's what I told her. That was my revelation, my secret. I spoke those words with all the sincerity at my disposal. I just couldn't do more. Too embarrassed, too guilty, too worried about upsetting my future wife. Now that I was committed, there was no need for terrible honesty. I was protecting her and, of course, I was protecting myself.

Millie said, "Oh, really," as if she was expecting more.

"I never touched her," I said truthfully. "But if this information makes you uncomfortable, Millie, I will let her go." I was willing to sacrifice Tanya to make Millie feel totally at ease.

"Oh, no, Dean," she answered. "You don't have to do that. I trust you."

Now I got right up on her—eyeball to eyeball, like a salesman closing a specious deal. "You have been so honest with me, baby. So honest it scares me a bit. But that's a big part of love, sharing the things you'd share with no one else. It just makes me love you even more." I put my hands on her shoulders. "No recriminations," I promised.

"No recriminations," she agreed.

Millie curled up in my arms. I kissed her forehead. I went back to sleep. All was right with my world.

FROM: ALADY27@EARTHLINK.NET

TO: CEESEE@HOTMAIL.COM

SUBJECT: GOOD-BYE

I told my fiancé about you last night and he took it well. Much better than I expected. Which makes it easier for me to do what I have to do now. If I'm gonna be a good mate, I can no longer have such an intimate relationship with another man. It's always hard to end a relationship, even one as hi-tech and strange as digital dialogue. You are like no other man I've been in contact with. I've shared parts of my mind with you that no one else knows exist. I will miss you. But, I must add, do not contact me again. Sorry, but this is what's best.

FROM: SEECEE@HOTMAIL.COM

TO: ALADY27@EARTHLINK.NET

SUBJECT: DEAN & MY WIFE

I wish our good-bye could be sweet. I wish we could end this with soft, saccharine words of affection, but I have some things to show you. They will be painful for you to watch. They are images of your fiancé. They are images of my wife. I got these images by accident. By accident I mean I didn't intentionally mean to get your Dean Chance on camera. I was definitely spying on my wife. He was with her. So he is on tape too.

Opening the attachment to this e-mail will change your life. Our relationship was built on honesty—don't you wish everyone else could say the same?

Chapter 24

Life is a constant balancing act. Whenever something great happens in your personal life, something sad happens in your professional life. Or things happen in reverse. The greater the public praise, the deeper the private torture. I've always tried to live my life without too many highs and surely as few lows as possible. Somewhere in the middle of life is a path of stability that keeps you out of jail, the nuthouse or any of life's major man-made tragedies.

Since Millie's return, I'd been traveling on a sweet wave of satisfaction and commitment. It had really been as harmonious a time as I've ever had with a woman, and I was looking forward to many more years of it. Bee was a memory—a great one to have stored far away.

I figured the certainty of my life with Millie was my reward for the craziness with Bee. I was foolish. The truth was, I'd enjoyed Bee so much and was so comfortable with Millie, a big nasty smack upside the head was due me. And it was gonna sting.

The hand of fate began its backswing one night as I was standing in the wings of *The Nick Shaw Show* next to a monitor as Shaw encountered the women of music video. Tendra and Kendra, two buxom, long-legged dancers who always worked together, were wearing dresses left over from their last gynecological examination. They acted and spoke as you'd expect from video dancers. The third woman, Kate, was another story. She was wearing a stern, polished air and a pants suit that said "Don't mess with me." She looked very familiar to me, but I couldn't place her.

Nick Shaw sat in his usual chair with the typical button-down shirt, upright posture and curious gaze that defined him on air. Despite the topic, he'd maintained the dignity of the show. But when he announced, "Wow, Tendra, it must get hot on those sets," I wanted to throw up.

"Let me tell you," she replied. "Just like these lights here on your show, they make you sweat."

"But," Kendra chimed in, "right now we're just sitting here. Now imagine we're on this hot-ass set dancing in little outfits all damn day."

Kate just sat there, looking vaguely disgusted by the conversation. I shared Kate's classy disdain.

"Yeah," Nick said with unearned earnestness, "I can imagine that."

"Oh," Tendra announced, "it gets funky in there."

"Funky?" Nick said. "It sounds fishy to me."

Kendra said, laughing, "Oh, my God, he didn't."

"Oh, yes he did," Tanya mumbled as she came up next to me.

"That was unnecessary, wasn't it?" I said.

"This whole segment is," she said firmly. "At least that girl Kate has some dignity."

"I didn't think Nick would go this route," I observed.

"Like my daddy said, once you get turned out, it's hard to put your pants back on."

"I don't remember you sayin' it like that, but the point's well taken. How's our token intellectual doing?"

"Oh," she said with excitement, "he's going to raise the level of this show. Plus, he's smart and he's cute."

Back on the set, Nick began his wrap. "Well, this has been a most entertaining segment. Next up: an author who thinks sexy videos do society good." Then he cut Kendra a leer and added, "Right now I'm inclined to agree. We'll be back in a minute."

The studio audience applauded with surprising enthusiasm. Our normally stuck-up group seemed to have enjoyed itself.

Tanya went to get our intellectual guest, and I walked over to intercept Kendra, Tendra and Kate. With a big toothy smile I said, "Great segment, ladies."

Tendra and Kendra gave me their basic fake, flirtatious "Thank you's" reserved for leering guys like me. But Kate paused a moment.

"You're Dean Chance, right?"

"Yes, I am. Sorry we didn't get a chance to meet before the show."

She said, "We've met before," then added, "Well, we didn't actually meet, but we've encountered each other before."

"Really?" I said. "That sounds mysterious. But you do look familiar."

"Yeah, Dean, we have a mutual friend."

Music video girl. Bee was a director/producer. Surely it was her. But I wasn't gonna say her name. I was gonna be as coy as

Kate. So I just asked, "Like who?" Kate smiled and said, "Think about it, Dean," and then, to my disappointment, walked away. I was gonna go after her when Tanya came down the hall with our "intellectual" guest. As he walked past Kate, they exchanged a sharp look but said nothing. "Professor Lawson," Tanya said, "this is my boss, Dean Chance. It's time you two met."

Finally I meet our ribald expert on debauchery. The Professor was a fortyish man with a Michael Jordan smooth head, a wide, powerfully built upper body that suggested he put in as much time in the weight room as the classroom, and a thin, sinister goatee. I had to admit there was something intimidating about this scholar. It wasn't just that his smile was sharp, designed to cut into the soul of the weak-willed. It wasn't just that he had a vise-like shake that seemed designed to take the measure of my strength. Something intangible—a touch scary and quite sexual—emanated from him.

"Thank you for coming on tonight," I said professionally. "I know you'll add a lot to tonight's program."

"I intend to, Mr. Chance," he said with a late-night voice that I imagined made coeds squirm. "I believe I can add some new elements to your night."

"Hopefully," I said with a plastic, make-him-feel-comfortable laugh, "you'll add them to the show too."

In perfect, slightly disrespectful deadpan he replied, "That's not a problem."

The stage manager came over. "We need to mike you, Professor Lawson. Please follow me." Lawson cut me an insolent smile and strolled over to the set.

"What's with him?" I asked Tanya.

"Come on, Dean. You know he's just professionally provocative."

Tanya had a book in her hand and offered it to me. The title was *Sexual Seeing: The Impact of Music Video on Our National Morality*. The author's name was C. L. Lawson.

"Just what does C.L. stand for?"

"C.L.? I'm not sure. Why, Dean?"

"I don't know."

I headed to the control room so I could look at monitors that provided various angles on Nick, Lawson and the crowd. Tanya was right about Lawson. The man worked hard at causing a ruckus. "So," Nick was saying, "you really believe the sexual imagery of music videos plays a healthy role in our society?"

"Sex is one of the few mysteries left, Nick," Lawson said with a sly, cocky sneer. "What goes on between two or more people in the privacy—"

"Two or more?"

"Sometimes."

"We need to hang out."

Nick was pleased with that little laugh-generating line but his guest was after a baser response. Lawson followed up, saying, "My point is, what goes on in sex happens behind closed doors. It's something we can speculate about, imagine and fantasize about. But we really don't know. I don't know what you do—you don't know what I do."

"Well," Shaw observed, "if it involves you and two or more people, I am rather curious." Lawson was bringing out the best in Shaw. I gazed at the audience monitor and saw many fascinated faces. Good television, I thought.

"You see, Nick," Lawson said in reply, "through music, we

can feel sexuality, we can feel fornication. It's in the grooves. It speaks to our intangible lust. The video, as an extension of music, puts undulating flesh to those grooves. It puts our deeply felt, unspoken fantasies in motion."

"That's a lot of weight to lay on a Puff Daddy video, Professor."

More laughter for Nick. Lawson seemed slightly irritated, yet not ruffled. After all, he was guiding the interview where he wanted it to go. Shaw was just counter-punching off his lead.

"But he, and all-important performers, carry it well, Nick. Let me give you a concrete example: I know a director who gets all her music video ideas from listening to people's sexual fantasies."

"Close friend of yours?"

"We were close once," he said with a leer that made it clear they'd fucked like rabbits. "She doesn't do literal interpretations, but she uses the kernel of their fantasies to tap into our collective desire."

"Sounds sexy."

And then it hit me! C. L. Lawson was Bee's ex-husband! That chill was back—I felt it in my toes, my back, my ears and right down in my nut sack.

"It is sexy and so is she."

"What's this director's name?" Nick inquired.

"And phone number?" Lawson responded, generating laughter from the studio audience.

Now it was Lawson with the laugh line and in total command.

"We can discuss that later," Nick countered. "But her name, please."

"Bee. She goes by the name of Bee."

I stopped breathing. I might never have breathed again if Tanya hadn't tugged at my arm. "Dean," she said. I must have jumped ten feet.

"WHAT?"

"It's Millie on the phone. She says it's urgent. Are you alright?"

"I don't think so." I walked over to the console and picked up my line.

"Yeah, Millie," I said casually, "what's going on?"

"Get over here right away!" Her voice was hot.

"Millie, I am in the middle of a show. I will be there when the show's over."

"If you ever want to see me again, you'll come now." Click. She was gone and I was dizzy. I looked back at the studio monitors where Nick was wrapping up.

"Thank you, Professor Lawson, for coming on tonight. And I'd also like to thank Kendra, Tendra and Kate for stopping by. Until next week, this is Nick Shaw saying, 'Always remember, when you're asleep, someone else is working.' Good night."

After the show, everyone was ecstatic. "Good show, good show" floated around the room. The combination of sex appeal, humor and smarts had people kind of giddy. Me? I was moving toward the exit when Tanya intercepted me.

"See, Dean," Tanya said, sounding cocky. "I told you he would save the show tonight. He brought class and sex appeal to the segment."

"I guess" was all I could muster in reply.

"Listen, we're going out for drinks. You want to join us?"

"I would like to have a word with Mr. Lawson. But I have to make a run. I'll be there in an hour."

I knew I was through the moment Millie opened the door. Trying to play off my dread, I said, "Baby, what's wrong?" I tried to kiss her, but she sidestepped me and headed away. "Millie, talk to me." No reply. She walked over to her computer and pointed.

"This," she said bitterly, "was downloaded into my computer today."

I grabbed her arms and turned her toward me. "What the fuck is this about?"

"It's about your dick."

I looked down at the computer. In a box on her screen, a soundless image of Bee and me kissing in front of her building. Then there was a cut and there I was, naked, in the window of Bee's apartment. There was another cut and I was atop Bee, my butt undulating between her legs.

"I've been set up, Millie." It was weak, but it was true.

"Like that's supposed to mean something to me?" she said. "I don't care who shot this, I just care that the man I loved cheated on me."

I was mumbling now. "I'm sorry, Millie, and I know you don't believe me—"

"No need for that 'I love you' shit. I'm not in the mood." She walked to the door and opened it. "Go!"

"Is this it?" I stammered. "Just like that?"

"Just as easy as you fucked that woman—that's how easy it should be for you to leave."

Not having a reply, I just walked out the door. Millie slammed it shut.

I was now a character in some twisted film noir. My behavior had come back to squash me. There was nothing to say, really. My dick had dragged me down and that was all there was to it. Then my cell rang. I said, "Hello," sheepishly, as if I expected this to be another smack upside the head. And I was bracing for it this time.

"You really fucked up, Dean." It was a man's voice. Brooklyn accent. Hard on the vowels. Slightly rugged.

"Who's this?"

"Evander. You remember me, right? Bee's driver."

"Can we meet somewhere?"

"Joe's Pub on Lafayette in a half-hour."

FROM: ALADY27@EARTHLINK.NET

TO: SEECEE@HOTMAIL.COM

SUBJECT: YOUR TAPES

Your tapes have ruined my life!

There is no other way to describe the impact they've had on me. I've been crying and crying with rage and hurt. Dean lied to me and that hurts so much. But you knew it would. Makes me wonder why you downloaded them to me. You saw what your wife did. Even as you taped it, you saw it. You saw her fucking another man and you just pressed record. That's your trip, I guess.

But wasn't sending them to me just as malicious an act as Dean's lying and cheating? It was as if your disappointment over your wife had to be shared. You wanted me in pain too. I'm glad I know that Dean cheated on me, but I'm not sure you mean me any good either.

FROM: SEECEE@HOTMAIL.COM

TO: ALADY27@EARTHLINK.NET

SUBJECT: MEET ME

Unhappily I agree with you. It was a nasty thing to do. A mean move on my part. I guess misery does love company. That doesn't excuse me. I guess it just explains my action.

Can I somehow make this easier for you? Can we meet and talk? Things have gotten too deep for these messages. We need eye contact. You can only understand my feelings, my true intentions, face-to-face. After all, I was just following your advice. I followed my "heart" and look what happened.

Chapter 25

Lafayette Street, where West Village meets East, is dotted with trendy spots between Astor Place and East Fourth — the Vietnamese restaurant Indochine; the hot yoga center Jivamukti; the Public Theater, where the theatrical visionary George Wolfe runs the show, and, in the same building, Joe's Pub, a cozy, ultra-cool cabaret where downtown boho meets designer gear. I'd been a few times to catch some music, but the pretense of the place often turned me off. Tonight Lenny Kravitz was in a corner booth, wearing shades in the dim light as he chatted with two slender blondes. But the goatees and the leather pants and the turtlenecks didn't irritate me tonight, 'cause I was sitting on a sofa nursing a cognac with Evander as he explained to me the last few months of my life. ". . . So when her husband started disrupting the sets, I had her back. Up until then, I'd been a grip. After I threw him off once or twice, she offered me a full-time as her driver/bodyguard. Real nice cheddar too."

"Is Bee her real name?"

"Beatrice Lawson Jones. Bee works better in the music video world."

"So you let that writer guy crack your skull?"

"Yeah," he said gravely. "The motherfucker snuck me. Came up on the side of the car with a baseball bat. Won't happen again. Bee didn't wanna press charges, but the shit did freak her out. She thinks Christian is wildin' out because of you. He's followed her since they broke up and he's always sending her ill e-mails. And since she's so 'open,' he's seen his ex-wife do some wild shit." He let that comment sit there a moment and then added. "But, like I said, you must have touched some nerve in him."

"With her too?" I said hopefully. "Have I touched a nerve in her?" Evander looked at me like I was a medical specimen, one that had been poked and prodded into the proper reaction. He put down his drink. "Let's go ask her," he said.

Outside Joe's Pub we pushed through the small crowd of folks waiting to get into the bar. When we reached the curb, Evander stopped and looked into the distance.

"Where are we going?"

"Right over there." He pointed. My eyes followed his finger. On the roof of a building two blocks down, movie lights brightened the night sky. It wasn't that hot a night, but between Joe's Pub and the building, my forehead got moist and my underarms clammy. In the lobby were the apple boxes, wires and general clutter of a film production. Evander nodded to everyone like he owned the place. We shared an elevator up with a young woman wrapped in an outfit that looked like black liquid. It took me a minute to realize that I'd met her before.

The suddenly talkative Evander started kicking game to her. "How you doing tonight, darlin'?" he asked.

"I'm alright," she replied, shy and cute. It was that girl from the projects—the one who'd spied on Bee and me.

"This your first video?"

"Yeah, and I'm the female lead. My name is Syndee. I'm really a singer. The director? Bee? She's gonna pass my tape on to Missy Elliot or Russell Simmons. I'm just wearing this to get in the game, you know."

Evander gave her body a serious survey and said, "Syndee, looks to me like you're in the game already. My name's Evander."

She turned her attention to me. "Do I know you?"

"I don't think so," I said, "but congratulations on the gig."

Thankfully, the elevator opened up and we all walked out onto a roof as bright as a noonday sun. On an elevated platform a squadron of female dancers moved with militaristic precision to a funky track as the movie crew worked around them. Kendra and Tendra were up on the middle of the platform, shaking what they mama gave them. Pamlesha, acting as choreographer, shouted out instructions to the dancers as they moved from left to right. Kate, so regal on our show, marched by in jeans, sneakers and an assistant director's headset.

Evander guided me toward a cluster of people to the left of the platform. In the middle of this bunch, intensely watching two video monitors, was Bee. Her hair was pulled back. She had on glasses, a leather jacket, cargo pants and sneakers. Then she yelled, "CUT!"

The music stopped. The dancers stopped. Everyone turned toward her.

"Okay." She thought a moment. "We got this. Let's move on to the next setup."

Kate lifted a megaphone and bellowed, "Moving on! Let's get second team into positions."

Bee turned around and smirked at me. "Hello, Dean. Welcome to my world."

As people scurried to make Bee's wishes come true, we sat on the edge of the same elevated stage the dancers had just giggled across. Bee looked relaxed, more in her element on this set than even in the bedroom. But I had not come to praise her, understand her or kiss her ass.

"Bee, you used me."

"I heard you shout, Dean, but I don't believe I heard you complain."

"Listen, bitch," I said harshly, "you used me. This is my fucking life you're filming here."

She put her finger to my lips and said quietly, "Believe me, Dean, no one here would guess that this was your sex life."

"Okay," I replied, "you did your thing. I did mine. I guess I got what I deserved. Let's move on: Your ex-husband e-mailed video footage of us fucking to my fiancée."

"He was good on your show, wasn't he?"

Now she was toying with me, basking in my discomfort just as she had so many times before.

"Did you know he would do that?"

"I always knew he was capable of stuff like that, but he's really been surprising me lately."

"Millie and I were engaged."

"How nice for you."

"And now we're not."

"Because of the e-mail?"

"Because I got caught up with you."

"You're easily led, Dean."

"Fuck you."

Kate came within earshot and made eye contact with Bee. "Bee, we'll be ready in ten." Bee nodded and Kate winked at me and walked away. My anger must have touched Bee because, finally, she seemed to speak from her heart and not from her all-powerful director's chair. "Listen Dean, even if you hadn't had Christian on the show, I was going to call you anyway."

"Yeah, right."

"I was, Dean. Really."

"Why? You don't really give a damn about me."

"If I didn't care about you, Dean, you wouldn't be here, and you're here because there's something you need to know—Christian is determined to seduce your Millie."

"Don't fuck with me, Bee."

"Dean, I'm serious. Christian has been in contact with your woman for a while. But because of what happened between us, he no longer wants to just touch her mind. He wants her body too, and he's very persuasive."

"What have you got me into?" Now I was raising my voice and the crew, which before had just glanced our way out of curiosity, watched us, full of concern. "For once tell me the truth. All of it."

"Okay," she said and took my arm in an effort to quiet me. "Even though Christian and I are separated, we still communicate. I know Millie told him about you and your fondness for Godiva chocolates and a lot of other things too."

"What's that got to do with anything?"

"Christian thought that suggested you had imagination. He knows I like men with imagination."

"Like I said, you used me."

"Okay. Yes. I used you."

"Those may be the only honest words I've ever heard from you."

"Bee!" Kate was coming over like she was ready to crack the whip on her boss.

"I've got to go, Dean."

"Back to your world, huh?"

"I'll help you, Dean. I promise." Then with a wicked smile, she added, "I mean you're my muse. I can't let you down. Can I?"

Bee gave me a chaste peck on the cheek and then headed over to where her crew awaited by the edge of the roof. I stood transfixed as Syndee leaned against the ledge, while a buff young man stood next to her, shirtless and oiled up. I knew what was gonna happen next, so I left.

Chapter 26

It was mid-September yet still deliciously hot in Manhattan. No one wanted to obey the calendar. Women still wore lovely, bright summer dresses and sexy sandals. Men with loosened ties and linen suits ambled down the street watching the summer dresses, admiring the sandals and letting the sun roll across their faces. Near where I stood, a well-dressed, corporate-looking couple displayed their humanity by engaging in a frantic tongue dance.

I watched enviously as I held my cell like a Bible and dialed a number with a prayer. A very nonangelic voice answered, "Good afternoon, Campbell and Kaufman Financial Services. Millie Starks's office. Blanche Boyd speaking."

"Blanche, it's Dean again."

Blanche sighed. "Dean, I'm sorry, but Millie is not available."

"You mean not available for me."

"Dean," she said sadly. "I'm sorry, but as I've told you repeatedly—"

Her middle-aged, white New York–accented voice stopped abruptly and, in the background, I could hear Millie. I yelled out her name, like a man seeking a life raft. There was a pause and then: "Is this Dean again?" she asked, as she toyed with me.

"Millie, you know damn well it's me, and it's about time you talked to me."

"I'm getting a restraining order, Dean." She spoke with cold calm I'd never heard before from her.

Sounding as desperate as I felt, I said, "Millie, I love you."

Very politely Millie replied, "Drop dead, motherfucker," and then hung up on me.

As I held the cell, a bouquet of perfume filled my nose. I turned and that deliriously happy couple came right past me, holding hands, their bodies leaning toward each other as if drawn by gravity. It just made me sick.

That night in bed I played love songs. Sarah Vaughn. Johnny Hartman with John Coltrane. Stevie Wonder. Cassandra Wilson. Miles back when he still wore suits. Billie Holiday singing "Lover Man."

On this night, with the air conditioner blowing and its long hum playing alongside my CDs, I wanted to be caressed by choruses, licked by the swelling of voices, charmed by clever turns of phrase and relaxed by instruments that fondled like a lover. I wrapped myself in these songs like they were blankets.

At these moments I knew I loved Millie, the contentment of being with her and the certainty of life she guaranteed me. Her loyalty, her steadfastness and her desire for me are what made me feel worthy of love and, in truth, inflamed my ego like a torch.

But then the CDs ended, and in that fleeting time when they shifted from one to the other I saw the bareness of my apartment, its hard-earned bachelor ambience, its needy solo feel. And in those seconds, the moments the love songs were designed to cover up, I felt a yearning for Bee that ate at my gut and dined on my intestines. Maybe it didn't have to be Bee—but it had to be someone with a willful, dominating spirit that I could give my emptiness up to. I just wanted to yield like a chastened child and be led by the nose, by the hand, by the dick.

Millie was my follower; Bee was my leader. And at this moment I was smack in the middle, listening to love songs, in possession of neither them nor myself.

FROM: DCHANCE@SHAWSHOW.COM

TO: MJACKSON@CKFS.COM

SUBJECT: US

You won't see me or return my calls, so I'm hoping you'll at least read my e-mail. You have every right to be mad at me. I totally fucked up. It happened during that period you went away on your business trip. It may not mean anything to you, but that affair only made me realize how deep my love for you is. You saw how strong I was for you when you returned. I was—and I still am—clear about my love for you. I want to marry you more than ever.

This may not mean anything to you either, but I believe I was somehow set up. This Christian guy and his wife decided, for whatever reason, to destroy our relationship. I don't know if it's because he was jealous of me or just because that's what he and his wife do—just play with people's lives for fun. I don't know. I don't even really care. I just know I don't want them to win. Don't let them win, Millie. Talk to me.

FROM: MJACKSON@CKFS.COM

TO: DCHANCE@SHAWSHOW.COM

SUBJECT: RE: US

I don't know what to think, Dean. I'm very confused right now. Everything was going so well and now everything is crazy. Nothing is solid right now. I thought you would be, but you're not. I mean, I don't even know who you are anymore. I opened up myself to you. I showed you sides of me I never had before. I was changing from having secrets to being as open as I could be. You said you had nothing to hide, no secrets, yet you had a secret bigger than any of my fantasies because it was real sex with real sweat and real sperm. It hurt me and it made me jealous too! So leave me alone, Dean. I don't wanna see you right now. Maybe I'll feel different someday. But right now, stay away from me. I just need to see things more clearly before I speak to you—if I do speak to you—again.

Chapter 27

After I hit bottom, after I'd sweated through sheets and watched soap operas and cried a few times, I did what always gets me through depression—I went back to work. Back in my office I had a role, a place and enough busy-work to free my mind. In fact my whole attitude changed as I made lists of potential guests, stuck up my index cards and surfed the Internet for subjects and ideas. Basically, for a time I suspended my personal life, trying to void my mistakes by erasing desire from my day-to-day life.

Besides, the show was now a certified pop phenomenon. Ratings were way up. Ad rates had been hiked with no protest from advertisers. That young male demo was watching. Shaw was being profiled in *New York*, *Newsweek* and *People*. In an office of happy people I smiled blandly, avoided personal conversations, though it was quickly common knowledge around the copy machine that my engagement had ended. With the aid of the ever-eager Tanya, I did my part to make the Shaw machine run. The new mantra at *The Nick Shaw Show* was "Let's keep it going!" which is why I got an unexpected visitor.

"So," Nick Shaw said as he walked into my office, "what

you got cooking, Dean?" I looked up from my computer screen and was quite surprised to see my boss standing in front of me. Shaw rarely came down to my end of the world—certainly not to ask about possible bookings.

"What happened?" I volleyed back. "You lost? Your office is down the hall, fella. The big one with the tall, attentive blonde sitting outside."

"I know the place," he said, looking up at my corkboard. "That looks good." He pointed to one of the cards. "Tell me more about it." I turned to see what had caught his eye and then explained, "Looks like you white folks are whipping up on your mates more often than we people of color."

Shaw pulled off the clipping that was tacked next to the card on the wall. "'Killings of black men by black women have fallen seventy-four percent in the last two decades,'" Shaw said, reading aloud. "Well, should you marry Millie, you have a very good chance of survival, Dean. It must be comforting."

"Read on, boss."

Shaw did and his brow furrowed. "Well," he said finally, "the number of white women killed by their husbands and boyfriends has risen over the last two decades. Seems I have a great chance of outliving my future wife in any major domestic dispute." He stuck the clipping back on the wall and then looked at another card. "Whiskey police?"

"You will not believe this," I began. "Bar owners are now hiring these guys to check up on 'shrinkage,' which is a euphemism for bartenders siphoning off liquor, by overpouring, giving out too many freebies, ringing up expensive brands, then pouring a cheaper bottle, and pocketing the difference, or simply serving drinks they don't ring up."

Nelson George

"I'm impressed with your grasp of bar larceny, but do you think this is a segment?"

"Not unless I come up with a strong angle. But just the idea of drink detectives is fun. Maybe I can link it up with other types of unusual law enforcement."

"That's an idea."

"So," I said and then waited.

"So," Shaw replied.

"You wanna know where the sex segments are?"

His telegenic, toothy, unembarrassed smile parted his talk-show-host lips. "You know me too well, Dean."

"I sure hope that's not true." From under my desk I slid out the small corkboard and laid the mini-board on my desk. Shaw came over looking hungrily at it. "What's this?" he asked, pointing at a card with the photo of an Asian woman tacked next to it.

"Zhou Weihui is the author of *Shanghai Baby*, a book that got banned in China because it was filled with sex, drugs and sex. It was a bestseller and a bit of a cultural phenomenon. The government blasted this lady as 'decadent, debauched and a slave of foreign culture.'"

"Sounds like our kind of guest," he agreed. "Can we get her?"

"I'm talking to some people at the State Department and there's a chance we can have her by December."

"So far so good. Quality yet nasty."

"You say that but you have a very unsatisfied look on your mug, Mr. Shaw."

"I have it often these days."

178

"Me too."

"Ratings are up. Ad rates are up. My profile is up."

"Yeah," I agreed. "And we've been blasted in the *Times* twice recently—in the Arts and Leisure and on the Op Ed page."

"But I can still get on *Charlie Rose*, and *New York* magazine is talking about a cover."

"So . . ."

"So we need to keep it up. Sweeps is coming and I need a juicy show or two. I want them to be as good as the music video show. Remember that one?"

"Can't forget that night."

"Too bad that Christian guy resigned his consultant's post. He was really helpful, wasn't he?"

"Oh, yeah," I said. "He did things you wouldn't believe."

Shaw didn't pick up on what I said, ignoring my comment by stating, "So, Dean, I need you to come through for me. I need something edgy yet smart. But you know that better than me."

"Making you happy makes me happy. By the way, what happened with you and the music vide-ho's?"

"Ho-ho-ho," he said. His exit line was "Wouldn't you like to know?"

I was putting my sexual corkboard back under my desk when Tanya entered. "Nick seems to be in a very good mood," she said, looking very much like a woman who had just been flirted with.

"Apparently he is happy."

"But you're not, are you?"

"How could I be?"

"I'm sorry she broke off your engagement. I'm sure she'll come back to you."

Lying badly, I answered, "I am too."

"Dean, I think I've come across something perfect for the show."

"What do you have?"

"Annie's."

"The musical?"

"The private party."

Chapter 28

Most days and nights Annie's was a regular bar/restaurant with bistro food, a decent wine list and a wide selection of cigars. It looked like one of the many faux-French joints that had sprung up around town in the last few years. Annie's was as ordinary as it could be except for an extremely private party held there once a month. There were no ads for it in the newspapers. Nor were there any flyers or press releases. If you knew about ScarletLetter.com and were curious, you could RSVP, but it was fifty dollars per person, so you had to be real curious to join in. Mostly you found out about Annie's by word of mouth passed from one swinger to another.

Tanya told me she'd discovered it on the Web. I knew Christian had played some role in Annie's uncovering but I didn't wanna know what or how they communicated. I hoped, though surely in vain, that Tanya didn't know much about Bee, Christian and me, and how they'd conspired to end my engagement. Tanya didn't ask; I didn't tell. The Professor had, wisely, quit working for us right after his on-screen appearance, citing his heavy class load and the new book he was writing. I often wondered what chapter I'd show up in.

All this was on my mind the night Tanya and I traveled down to Annie's. It was located in the Wall Street area, which on the weekend is empty of street traffic and as ghostly as the echo of money lost and gained. As we walked up to the door, a white couple came up beside us. She was a comely bottle blonde with big blue eyes and large breasts; he was a stocky, weight lifter type in a boxy gray suit. They appeared quite suburban, very married and extremely eager to make friends. "Hey, how are you guys this evening?" He was Tom Kastanzi and she was Bonnie Kastanzi of Edison, New Jersey.

We must have seemed unnerved by their enthusiasm. "Don't be nervous," Bonnie said reassuringly. "Everyone here is so nice."

From the alcove at the front of Annie's I could see the interior was burnished browns and golds, like any good drinking room, and I could hear the music of Maxwell's first album floating through like a fog. On a big blackboard menu by the front door, "Welcome Lovers" was written in pink and blue pastel chalk. A white man with the face of a cherub, peanut brown hair and a most accommodating manner greeted the Kastanzis by name and then turned his attention to us. "Good evening. Welcome to Annie's. I'm your host, Pete Stairs. And you are?"

"I'm Tanya Chance and this is my husband, Dean. We spoke on the phone?"

"Yes, we did," Pete said, his cheeks bright like cherries. "So glad you could make it." He led us over to a table where Nance, a robust, very pale woman with an earthy voice and thick reddish hair, sat with a cash box and a ledger. After we'd signed in and put fifty dollars apiece in the kitty, the Jersey couple immediately offered to buy us drinks. "That's a great idea," Pete said, cutting in, "but just let me speak to Mr. and Mrs. Chance for a moment."

"No problemo," Tom replied, "but we want our drink before it gets too busy in here."

"Absolutely," Tanya answered as the Kastanzis moved inside and Pete's accommodating manner hardened. "Mr. Stairs, this is my boss, Dean Chance. I've briefed him on your ground rules."

"That's right," I said in my most official-sounding tone. "We will not identify ourselves as media people. We will not approach anyone about being interviewed. Anyone we're interested in, we'll tell you and you'll make the contact."

"Yes, that's how it's got to be."

"No question about that," I said, shifting to kiss-ass mode. "We respect everyone's right to privacy."

"Good." Pete was still a touch nervous around the eyes. "People in the swing world have to protect each other. Some of us could lose our jobs if it ever got out. This is not a frivolous undertaking. It's a serious life choice. I've seen your show. I like what you're doing in expanding the horizons of sexual discussion in the mainstream, so I'm allowing you in. But discretion is the only way this works."

"Absolutely," Tanya chimed in on cue and Pete guided us inside. Now, if you didn't know people were here to find another couple (or couples) to have sex with, it would have looked like nothing more than an eclectic gathering of thirty-ish adults. A DJ played mellow makeout music as the mostly white crowd bantered quietly. There were a few interracial couples on the fringes (black man and white woman, Asian woman and white man), but biracial Tanya and I were the closest thing to black-on-black action in the house.

At Annie's, people were living the down-low life, all of them conspiring to add something extra, something fun, something sinful, to their lives, with their lifemates as willing accomplices. No secrets here—at least not within the relationship. They were all part of an extremely honest secret society. They lied to the world but not to each other. Guarded against the outside, yet naked to each other. Normal, within these walls, was whatever they decided it was. To most people this was a violation of their vows. To the customers here it was an enhancement of those very vows.

The Kastanzis intercepted us by the bar and immediately suggested we go upstairs with them. Tanya seemed nervous, but after being ordered around by Bee, played for a fool by Christian and dismissed by Millie, these Jersey folk hardly seemed threatening to me. On the next level was a lounge with a pianist tinkling "Stella by Starlight" on the ivories, a smaller bar where you could also order finger food and a series of curved couches I assumed were designed for multiple-choice activities. When we walked in with the Kastanzis, heads swiveled like conference room chairs. Apparently we were the freshest, most exciting new meat available, and people sniffed out our scent immediately.

After settling in with our drinks (Tanya and I each ordered a glass of Merlot, while Mr. Kastanzi went for straight whiskey and his wife had a Cosmopolitan), we told them that we were just curious, quite nervous swing club virgins. "Oh, I remember our first time," Mrs. Kastanzi said. "Don't you, Tom?"

"Yes, I do," he chuckled. "It was very embarrassing."

"Oh, Tom. It was your first time. That happens unless you're a real exhibitionist," she said, and then, with a stage whisper, added, "It just so happens that I am."

We truly had a live one here in Mrs. Kastanzi. So, under the guise of flirting, I pumped her for info: They'd been swinging for three years; it had been a fantasy of hers for years; he'd been reluctant until he saw how it enhanced their sex life; now they came to Annie's every month and frequented other clubs when their daughter was away at summer camp, as she was now.

As Mrs. Kastanzi rattled on, the couples on the couch across from us slowly, with the subtlety of a summer breeze, exchanged partners. It happened softly—a shift in posture, hands rubbing shoulders, a caress, eyes linked by invisible strings. And then they all stood up and moved through a door I hadn't noticed before.

"Where's that lead to?"

Mrs. Kastanzi smiled, shy as a baby deer, and explained, "It takes you up to another, more intimate lounge. Do you wanna take a look?"

"Is it alright?" I asked.

I glanced over at Tanya and Mr. Kastanzi, who was sharing his photos from his last fishing trip off the Jersey coast.

"Oh, yeah. This is how it usually works."

Tanya looked up as we stood. I told her, "We're just gonna go look around." Mr. Kastanzi didn't seem concerned as his buxom wife took me by the arm and steered me through the new door and up a stairway illuminated by three crimson bulbs. Low pulsating electronic music throbbed in the air. A white couple huddled against a stairway wall, their mouths sucking each other like two babies sharing one nipple.

"Some people meet and go to another bar," she explained. "Others go to someone's apartment or a hotel. Those that feel instantly drawn to one another come up here."

At the top of the stairs was another door. "Don't feel obligated to do anything," Mrs. Kastanzi told me as she rubbed a soft hand against my butt. "It's your first time, after all." Through the door was a room lit by tiny purple-tinted bulbs. That insistent music was now remixed by the wet, slithering sound of bodies undulating, moist skin against moist skin. It took a minute for my eyes to adjust and then I could see naked people. Not all of them beautiful. Only a few sleek and chic. Yet all of them exploring their dream of controlled promiscuity.

Scattered about the rubber mats were clothes, drinks, condom wrappers, tubes of lubricant, earrings, a dildo or two, and what might have been someone's wedding band. As I watched, I could feel Mrs. Kastanzi's hands—all twelve of them—coiled around me like old-fashioned bedsprings, all of them ready to bend, squeak and bounce, bounce, bounce.

My fly was open and Mrs. Kastanzi was poking around lazily when I saw a salt-and-pepper duo of women on either side of a black man's torso. It wasn't the dude from downstairs. Yet something about the face was familiar. As the pepper woman kissed his nipples and the salt woman pleased his neck, I saw the grinning face of Christian, his eyes closed and his body naked, his dick quivering with anticipation like a stick in the wind.

"Don't worry about him, Dean," Mrs. Kastanzi said, the stage all out of her hoarse whisper. "He's always showing off. I know you measure up."

All I could do now was think of Millie. My eyes darted around the darkness. Was that butt familiar? Did I know that breast? Did someone cry out in that high, happy way I've savored these past few years? My eyes answered every question "NO!" even as the salt-and-pepper duo moved to Christian's groin as joyously as a child does to a Christmas tree.

"You alright, Dean?" It was Mrs. Kastanzi, clearly disappointed at the sudden downward direction of my desire. I pried myself free from her arms and walked out of the room. Coming up the stairs was Mr. Kastanzi and Tanya.

"What's wrong, Dean?"

"I have to go, Tanya."

"Should I come with you?"

"No. Talk to some more people. Get some more stories. I just have to go."

"What's upstairs, Dean?"

I didn't stop to answer. As I went down I heard Mrs. Kastanzi mention something like "Dean certainly is competitive, isn't he?" and I just moved faster.

I wanted to be as open and as bold as Mr. and Mrs. Kastanzi, but right now I wasn't ready for it. I was too lonely, too jealous, too confused. I sat in my car and began to wonder whether that was Christian or not. Maybe I just didn't want to admit that Christian's dick was bigger than mine. Maybe I didn't wanna see what I was seeing—Christian playing his instrument for Millie.

Now I had a new nightmare. Christian doing everything to my woman I'd done to his. Before I knew it I was outside on the barren streets of the financial district vomiting. One or two emasculated tears, like those of an aging athlete feeling the game had passed him by, dropped to the sidewalk. As I held my stomach and leaned my head against a stone wall, I mumbled, "Millie, Millie, Millie," as if she could hear my dumb ass.

Chapter 29

The last week of September but it still felt like August. The heat baked the garbage. The tar that covered the streets was soft and spongy. Deodorant was a joke. I existed in a gray, dingy funk, feeling as fresh as the soles of a beat cop's feet. I'd stopped calling Millie. Bee had never called. The video of my ultimate sexual fantasy showed up on MTV, looking as silly as it deserved to.

Yet at my job I was a hero. Integrity had long ago slipped away. Ratings kept going up. The syndicator was ecstatic. It was all my fault and I had a spanking new raise to prove it. So I sat in a conference room on a sweltering day as Walker, our corporate liaison, presented us with a new plan for world domination: "We know that some may see this as a radical departure, but we believe it could finally shore up the show's one demographic weakness. What do you think, Nick?"

"Well, we started as a public affairs show that got good reviews and so-so ratings. I was fine with that. But," he said, glancing at me, "there's nothing wrong with continuing to raise our ad rates. If this will do that, I'm open."

"A female sidekick?" I wondered with sarcasm. "What are we talking here—Ed McMahon with breasts?"

"I think I dated her," Nick quipped, and I knew it was a done deal. Still I tried again to shoot it down.

"It sounds like the *Howard Stern Show*, guys."

"Look, Mr. Integrity," Nick replied, "it was your idea to do the women of music video show."

"What? Is that the scarlet letter?"

"Hardly, Dean. It just means Pandora's out of her box and I gotta say, Dean, she's looking good to me."

"We can't just turn back into a calm public affairs show, you know, if this doesn't work."

"Dean, I have no interest in going back." Nick's eyes were dancing now, like a tab of Ecstasy had just kicked in. "I'm loving getting dirtier, a little racier. Besides, you know what this means?"

I knew. I knew. "Auditions for your cohost, Nick?"

"And that's why you're my producer, Dean."

I didn't know it was this simple: You alter your personal life and, eventually, it changes your business. It was a chain reaction: Millie goes away; Bee and I play; I embrace Millie without reservation; and my lie bites my ass. All I got out of it was some beautifully busted nuts, a painful loss and enhanced ratings. Back in the office, my eyes on *MTV Jams* while I contemplated my decisions, I didn't notice when Tanya walked in and sat across from me.

"Dean?" she said quietly.

I said, "Yeah," staring at Ananda on the tube.

"I need to talk to you."

"Go ahead."

Her voice turned imploring. "Dean, it's really important."

Finally I looked over at her. My assistant's face was long and drawn. Eyes a little baggy. Man problems. No question. "Oh, shit," I replied, "it's gonna be complicated, isn't it?"

"I've got a situation, Dean," she said haltingly. "It's of a personal nature. It involves that man we had on the show — Christian Lawson."

Now, of course, she had my full attention. I urged her to continue. "Well, we've become close, Dean." Oh my God, she fucked him! "He's so smart and so sexy and, well, I've never met anyone like him. He e-mails me every day. And the things he tells me and asks me . . ."

The poor thing was blushing, which, for some reason, irritated the hell out of me. I wanted to tell her to shut up and leave, but I bit my tongue and just nodded as if I was sympathetic.

"It's great, really, except, well, he wants me to do something I've never done before."

"Really?"

"It's not like I'm a prude or anything but . . ."

Now I was really pissed, probably because on some level I was jealous of his conquest of Tanya. It scared me too. Christian was still around me — still in my world. So I said, "Tanya, why are you telling me if it's this personal? It is none of my business."

"Well, I don't know, Dean — it might be." Now she really was embarrassed. Tanya was firebox red. Her words came out in a dribble, like a sad child caught cheating. "You see, Christian wants us to make love to Millie. Oh, I said it. I can't believe I said it, but there it is."

Life was just never to be right again, was it? That day at Barneys I walked through an entrance to hell and Christian was the damned devil. I just looked at Tanya and said nothing. "Well . . ." She waited patiently. "What do you think?"

Finally I said, "Is this something you want to do?"

"Well, to be honest, Dean, I always thought Millie was very cute." Tanya saw she'd gone too far with that one and added, "Not that this was my idea, Dean. Christian suggested it and it's really about him, you know. I want to show him that I'm not a liar."

"A liar?" I said.

"Oh, Dean," she replied. The girl was on the edge of tears. "I should tell you everything, shouldn't I?"

"What," I asked through clenched teeth, "is there to tell, Tanya?"

"Back in the spring I attended this seminar down in the Village on sexuality and progressive thought. It was at the New School."

"Yeah?"

"And Professor Christian Lawson was a speaker."

"This was before you recommended him to be a consultant on the show?"

"Yes, I knew him before then. When you mentioned the consultant job, I went to him about it and at first he was reluctant. He doesn't like to be in situations where he has no control."

"Go on," I said, uttering those two simple words with dead seriousness.

"I befriended him that night, but since he was married, I didn't mention him to you and anyone else."

"Befriended, huh? You are really quite something, Tanya."

"There's more, Dean, and I'm afraid it'll really upset you."

I laughed, if you can call the bitter sound that passed my lips a laugh. "Okay, Tanya, thanks for sparing my feelings, but I think you better just bring all you got."

"Well, Millie was at the seminar too."

"Millie was at this New School seminar?"

"Yes, she was, so when Christian gave out the address of his Web site and chat room, she must have written it down. I believe that's how they hooked up. I know they kept in contact because he would ask me things about her."

"And about me too, Tanya?

"Yes, Dean."

My brain felt like it was being ground up in a blender and all my understanding of life and how things worked were getting sliced like so many pieces of fruit. "All of which leads to you, the Professor and Millie, right?"

"Oh, Dean." Tanya was still upset and I was surely at the end of my patience. "Christian got me to write down my sexual fantasies. He said it would liberate me. Well, I wrote about having a ménage à trois and he said he could make that happen. It was gonna be freaky anyway, but bringing Millie into it makes it weird."

My voice was bone dry, but I still asked, "Does Millie wanna do this?"

"He says we'll meet tonight to discuss it." Tanya was still waiting on me to truly respond. Maybe this was all a trick to get me to react? Another mind-fuck of stupid-ass Dean Chance? "What do you think, Dean?" Tanya asked. "Please, Dean, what do you think?"

FROM: ALADY27@EARTHLINK.NET

TO: SEECEE@HOTMAIL.COM

SUBJECT: OUR MEETING

Just confirming our meeting tonight. I'll be there but, as you know, I have my limitations. Don't rush me. Just let me feel it out, OK? See you at eight.

FROM: SEECEE@HOTMAIL.COM

TO: ALADY27@ EARTHLINK.NET

SUBJECT: NO PROBLEM

No problem. Your choice. You have control. But I guarantee you something you've never seen before.

Chapter 30

That night humidity hung in the air like in a dank, old-style brick sauna. Oppressive and all-engulfing, the heat affected every fiber, and every limb of every living thing in town. The cars ran hotter. The tempers ran shorter. Every quick movement required long, breathy moments of recovery. Summer in New York was a beautiful thing. But now it was almost Halloween and the city was slowly suffocating in this unprecedented heat wave. Brownouts were common. Con Edison had become a curse word. There were restrictions on water use. People were wearing flip-flops on Wall Street.

So when Tanya walked on this sticky, moist night, she did so slowly, almost languidly. This wasn't the perky, bright-eyed little assistant who moved through our professional, air-conditioned environment. This was an undulating young woman in a pastel summer dress with a light glow to her skin and the self-conscious gait of someone who knew she was being watched.

Tanya came upon the restaurant and stopped a moment, looking in the window, before entering. She spoke with a waitress and then sat down at a table right near the restaurant's front window. Then she looked out of it, not smiling, as I tapped my hand on the steering wheel.

I turned to my companion and said, "I grew up near here."

"I know," Evander said evenly. "Remember?"

Evander watched the restaurant too. There was an aluminum baseball bat in his lap.

"You know," I suggested, "you could kill him with that if you're not careful."

"Oh, I'll be careful," Evander replied. "If I have to kill him, it'll be with this." He pulled an old-school revolver out of his jacket.

"What are you gonna do with that?"

"The gun is just a persuader," he explained. "It gets him in the car. The bat is for my amusement."

"There she is," I said. My ex-fiancée came down the same street Tanya had, but her dress was shorter and her legs were bigger, and her walk a little more strident. Tanya walked like she had something to prove; Millie strode like she was the proof.

"Damn," Evander exclaimed. "No wonder you're so upset. Baby got back."

That got no response from me. I just sat silently as she entered the restaurant.

Through the front window I saw a sheepish Tanya wave her over. Millie walked to the table and they greeted each other with kisses on the cheek. Millie sat down and immediately they started chatting.

"Looks like your woman and your assistant are with it, Dean," Evander said slyly. "Now don't you wish you'd suggested it?"

Again I didn't respond. I just watched and drummed my

fingers on the steering wheel. Time passed. It got hotter. The radio played that song Bee made the video for, which made Evander chuckle. My mood darkened as Millie and Tanya sat drinking sake and laughing.

"Yo, man," Evander said at one point, "they feelin' each other."

Somehow I got the baseball bat from Evander and started squeezing the barrel. I was having evil thoughts when I looked in the rearview mirror. "Shit."

"What's up?" he asked.

As I slumped down I replied, "Look."

Coming down the street behind us, holding hands and looking lovey-dovey, were Nick Shaw and the dancer Pamlesha. Now we both slumped down in our seats as they walked in front of the car and then headed across the street. They too entered that same Japanese restaurant.

Evander said, "Somebody has a serious party planned."

Through the window we saw Shaw and Pamlesha walk over to Millie and Tanya, where introductions were made. They too sat down.

"Are you sure Christian's coming?"

I told him, "That's what Tanya said."

"I don't know, Dean," Evander replied. "He's a jealous-hearted guy. When he orchestrates his personal parties, he's usually the only dog in the pound. Nick Shaw being here seems out of character."

Through the front window, I saw Millie answer her cell phone. She listened, clicked it off and stood up. Shaw shook his head as if to say "I'll pay for your dinner." She kissed him on the cheek and headed for the door.

"She's leaving," I said, stating the obvious.

"Well, you better follow her, then."

"You're not coming?"

"Something's up with this right here," he said with a leer. "Anything Pamlesha's down with is worth waiting for."

"What about Christian?"

Millie exited the restaurant and headed down the street.

"There's an awful lot of pussy in the air," he said. "Christian will show up someplace."

Evander got out of the car and I pulled away, driving in Millie's direction. I was no detective, but I figured I could follow the woman I loved with no problem. I drove down Second Avenue like a snail, one hand on the wheel, one hand fingering Evander's baseball bat. Cars blew at me. Pedestrians cursed me. But I stayed a half a block or so behind her. If she heard the commotion I caused I couldn't tell, 'cause she kept moving straight ahead.

She was heading toward Professor Christian (aka C.L.) Lawson, who stood in front of a porno store, dressed impeccably in a blue seersucker suit that made him look ridiculously cool despite the sweltering humidity. He was smoking a cigar when she walked up to him. He hugged her but I noticed she turned her head when he tried to kiss her lips. At least that's how I interpreted things from the window of my slow-moving car.

My eyes, clearly, were not on the road. Nor was I driving very smoothly. Which is probably why a livery cab bumped into my rear with a loud, crunching noise. Both Lawson and Millie turned and saw me, so I gunned my engine and sped off. At the next corner I made a left and quickly double-parked my ride. The livery cab that had bumped me came up on my ass and a hefty, light brown Latino popped out.

"Hey, man," he shouted, "you need to learn to drive! You can't be stopping like that!"

I got out too—with the baseball bat in my hand. But it wasn't for him—unless he slowed me down. He stared at my bat, flinching a beat, as I walked by.

"Where you going, yo?" he asked. "We got to exchange information and shit."

I didn't stop walking. Over my shoulder, I said, "Leave it on my windshield," and then swung the bat with one hand, trying to wave him off. I heard him call me a "Crazy fuck!" but I had no time to argue. Back on Second Avenue there was no sign of Millie or Lawson. I looked around a minute and then went inside the porno store.

The cashier, a lanky kid with short, spiky hair and a Pantera T-shirt, looked at me and then at my bat. "Mister," he observed, "it's better to make love, not war." I didn't answer. I just walked in and looked around.

Magazines were stacked along both narrow walls according to categories of sexual desire. In the back were freestanding shelves filled with videos that reached up to the ceiling.

"Where are your booths?" I asked.

"Past the shelves?" the cashier said, now looking at me with concern.

"Did you see a man and woman come in here?"

"All the time," he said. I cut him a threatening look and he returned it. I headed down the aisle, feeling like a hunter, the bat tight in my right hand. I was moving between two shelves of tapes when I heard a woman's voice in the next aisle.

Clutching the bat in both hands, I turned too quickly around a corner and stumbled, knocking over some tapes, and came face-to-face with two women sporting short hair and tattoos. Both greeted me with withering stares.

"Excuse me," I said, and then I loosened my grip on the bat and headed backward down the aisle. There was no one in the next aisle, so I moved toward the back. There were three booths before me. It was like I was suddenly in *The Price Is Right* of porn. I opened door #1 cautiously. Empty. A bit emboldened, I moved to door #2 and flipped it open. Empty.

I knew they were behind door #3. I could feel someone in there. I was breathing heavily, both excited and fearful of what I'd see. I gripped the bat in my right hand and went to open the door with my left. I gathered myself and then pulled on the handle. This one was locked. I pulled again. "Open the goddamn door, Christian! I know you're in there!"

Hurried movements behind door #3. Guilty hands moving quickly. I stood back, ready to smash a fastball. Finally, there was the click of the latch. Door #3 opened. A white-haired elderly man right out of a retirement home looked wide-eyed at me and my bat.

"Sorry, bud," he said apologetically, "but this is my favorite booth too!"

Deeply mortified, I mumbled an apology and turned away, walking past the other booths, past the shelves of tapes and the two women, toward the open front door, through which I saw Millie standing on the sidewalk, looking as if in a dream. "MILLIE!" I yelled. She turned toward me, framed by the door like a painting. In a stride I moved toward her, past the porno mags, the cashier and the doorway, until reality bit in the form of two patrolmen on either side of the doorway. My bat fell to the sidewalk with a hollow clank.

"MILLIE! MILLIE!" I shouted, sounding silly.

One of the officers informed me, "Mr. Chance, you're under arrest!"

Standing behind the cops, greatly amused by the unfolding scene and still smoking that cigar, was Lawson. Next to him stood the livery driver, saying, "Yeah, that's that crazy punto!"

"Fuck you!" I screamed at Lawson. To Millie, who stood apart from us all, looking at me wet-eyed but disdainful, I said, "Millie, this man is a sick freak! You got to get away from him!" She didn't reply. She just watched me get handcuffed and stuffed into the back of a patrol car.

Chapter 31

I was back in the same room, sitting in the same chair, talking to the same two fun-loving detectives from my wicked night of rooftop sex.

"You know," Detective Toro observed, *"The Nick Shaw Show* has really changed lately. Women of music video. Russian strippers invade New Jersey. The private world of hip-hop hoochies."

Then Detective Anderson added, "And we'd wondered why the focus had shifted."

"Now, Mr. Chance," Detective Toro concluded, "we know."

"Have you guys been listening to me?" I pleaded. "This guy Christian Lawson is ruining my life."

Detective Toro explained, "There's nothing inherently illegal in a guy being upset at the man who's fornicating with his wife on rooftops."

"You mean his ex-wife?" I clarified.

Detective Toro had a laptop computer on the interrogation room table. He punched some keys and looked at the screen.

He said, "Well, Mr. Chance, according to the computers of the State of New York, Christian Lawson and Beatrice Jones Lawson are still married."

"Now," Anderson said, "they may be separated."

Detective Toro reasoned, "I guess if she's fornicating with you near a chimney in the projects, she probably is."

"Sounds right to me," said Detective Anderson. Then he continued, "But that wouldn't stop me from being angry at you, Mr. Chance."

Detective Toro picked up his point: "Stealing your girl and making a chump out of you are not illegal, Mr. Chance. And, I might add, it doesn't seem all that difficult."

This cracked them both up and I had to admit to myself, I wasn't looking or feeling too bright. After their laughter had died down, Detective Toro told me, "Mr. Chance, you have violated a restraining order, run from an accident scene and made several X-rated shoppers very nervous. By all rights you should be spending the evening telling this same wonderful story to your cell mates at central booking."

"But," Anderson interjected, "we're gonna let your sorry ass go home."

A very relieved "Really?" passed my lips.

"You are definitely being played for a sucker," Anderson said. "We know and understand that."

"Thanks," I said. "Thanks a lot."

"Plus," Toro added, "someone is outside waiting on you."

"Who?"

"You'll see, Mr. Chance," Detective Toro said. "But first we have some advice."

Detective Anderson asked me, "Did you know that almost seventy percent of all e-commerce was sex-related throughout the nineties?"

Then Detective Toro added, "And that at one point Pam Anderson's Web site received more hits than almost any in the whole world?"

"So you're saying I should just stay home and jerk off, and avoid rooftops?"

"Take the advice from two old-school surfers: It works for us." The two detectives laughed again and, since I was getting out, I felt comfortable laughing too.

When I exited the station a strong, cool breeze ran across my face, drying my sweat and cooling my temper. Instead of the anger that had coursed through me all night, I felt like my normal, all-too-reasonable self again. Which was good, since Bee, looking as glammed out as a Dolce & Gabbana ad, sat in the driver's seat of a blue Beemer. I strode over like we were actually friends.

"Did you know you were married?" I asked, polite as hell.

"Do tell," she replied with the icy edge she so easily summoned.

I leaned in real close to her and wondered, "How'd you know I was in there?"

"Evander called and said to check. He had a feeling you'd end up here."

"And where is your loyal retainer?"

"Let me give you a lift and maybe we'll run into him."

Bee looked like the ultra-confident, hypersexy lady I'd encountered last spring at Barney's. Was this a good thing for me? Shouldn't I just go home and get some sleep? My little internal debate was a joke. A minute after her offer I was riding in the air-conditioned cool of her Beemer, looking at her profile.

"So," she said too casually, "the New York City Police told you I was still married."

"Yeah," I said, looking away from her. "Who knew they could be so informative."

"Dean, open the glove compartment." Inside the glove compartment was a gun. I looked at it while she kept her eyes on the curves of Riverside Drive. "It's under the gun," she instructed. Her voice was too easy, too easy for comfort. "Look under the gun." Under the gun was a small bottle of CK cologne.

"See the Calvin Klein?"

"Yeah," I said, confused.

"Put some on. You need it."

I pulled out the bottle and splashed a handful on my neck and chest.

"Jail smell, huh?"

"That's right. We don't want any of these supermodels dancing with their noses pinched."

"Where are we going, Bee?"

"To see if your girlie will take you back."

Chapter 32

B ee found a spot on Sixty-eighth Street across from the Sony Lincoln Center and walked past the theater and around on Sixty-seventh Street to her apartment. I looked around as we walked, expecting to see a familiar face in a car or on a street corner. I waited for that cold chill—the one I understood now—to run through me. But all I felt was that same cool breeze from before, now coming across the West Side from Central Park.

In the lobby was that same doorman, the smiling witness to my countless seductions at Bee's hands. "Good evening, Bee," he said as always.

"Hi," she answered cheerfully, "it's good to see you again."

I walked right past the doorman but stopped when he said, "Excuse me, sir, are you on the list?"

"She lives here."

"No, Dean, I don't." She turned to the doorman and explained, "Yes, I'm on the list and he's my 'plus one.'"

The doorman surveyed the list and scratched off a name. "Okay," he said blandly. "Have a good time."

As we walked toward the elevator, I told her, "I know it's

taken me a minute, but I am finally getting the message: Nothing I know about you is true. Not that I know that much about you."

The elevator door opened and a stylishly dressed couple passed us. Once the doors closed, Bee got real close to me. "Well," she began, "you know I'm a great lover."

"And I assume you really do like men's feet."

"See," she said, still in character, "you do know things about me."

"But you don't live here?"

"No, Dean. I'm a downtown kinda gal."

When the elevator door opened, loud hip-hop filled the hallway. Bee took my hand and led me toward the noise. It was the same hallway we'd walked down so many times before, but it felt like I'd never, ever been here. "The place belongs to a friend," she explained. "He was out of town. We shot a video there and then I watched the place while he was away."

The apartment door opened and the music hit me full blast. As we entered, a tall, multiracial-looking woman spoke to Bee in French and then stuck out her tongue, which was very pierced. Bee pulled me past her. The rust-colored living room was jammed with people dancing barefoot in the sunken area. Other folks sat on that long, curved sofa talking, drinking, kissing and staring blankly into space.

Over by the huge blowup photo of rebounding hands was Evander, hugged up and exchanging soft kisses with Pamlesha. I tapped him on the shoulder.

"What?" an irritated Evander said and then turned his head. "Oh, Dean. How's it hanging, son?"

"What happened to you?"

"I followed them here and then intercepted this subject."

Pamlesha took exception to Evander's description.

"'Intercepted'?" she said and sucked her teeth. "Dean, you know me better than that. If there was any intercepting, I did it."

Evander, all soft and pliant, cooed, "We can call it anything you like, boo."

"Have you seen Christian?" I asked.

"I have to admit I've lost track of him, Dean, but if you see him, holla at me. Where's Bee?"

"Right here," I said, but of course she wasn't. I hadn't even felt her let go of my hand, it was so crowded in the room. Bee was gone. She'd blended into the maze of lovelies. All that beauty. It made me feel so desperate. Finding Bee was surely finding Lawson and finding Lawson, unfortunately, meant finding Millie. In a party like this you could lose two women and never find yourself. I turned to scan the crowd and found my face buried in the large, hard, silk-shirted back of a real big brother.

"Excuse me," I mumbled.

The man, disguised as a wall, turned, revealing his face and that of the person on the other side of him — Bee.

"Bee, I've been looking for you."

"Well, you found me," she said like I was a joke. "Meet Tony. This is his place. He spends half the year playing ball in Europe and the other half throwing fabulous parties."

"And," he said evenly, "with whatever time I have left over, I wonder what she's up to now."

"Tony, you're embarrassing me."

With a knowing smile, Tony replied, "Girl, I doubt that's possible." From his six-foot, ten-inch height, Tony looked down at me from his Olympian height, as if taking my pedigree. Then he leaned his long body down and whispered above the din. "A word of advice, son: Keep your jimmy tight and your dreams to yourself." Tony knew the deal.

"It's too late, Tony," I said, sensing a kindred spirit.

"Okay, son," he said, grinning. "See you on MTV."

Tony offered his fist. I touched it with mine. He kissed Bee on the cheek and moved on.

"What did Tony say to you?"

"Nothing I didn't already know." Then I saw something that made me say, "Damn."

Tanya was dancing wildly between a muscular black man in a tank top and gold chain and an athletic-looking woman I recognized as Kate, the assistant director. The couple was making a very willing sandwich of her twitching body.

"Oooh," Bee moaned, "that is a nice image."

Seeing Tanya brought back my sense of purpose. "Bee, take me to where Millie is."

As casual as she could, Bee answered, "Oh, Millie? Probably the bedroom with Christian."

I was pushing through the crowd, knocking into dancers, knocking over drinks, before I could even think. I left Bee behind me, though I felt that chill, like she was watching and enjoying my sudden frenzy.

The bedroom door was closed. I grabbed the knob and, in an instant, there was no music, no people, no other sound. Just my breathing, the click of the doorknob turning and the soft rub of the door's bottom against the rug. I slipped into the room, closing the door behind me and then gazed at the figure in the bed illuminated by the television. There was nothing else in the world.

The figure was a man—a naked man—who sat on the edge of the bed with his back to the door. He leaned forward with his head aimed at the television. I slowly walked toward him.

"Hey, babe, is that you? I'm almost ready now." He sounded pathetic—sick and whipped and worried. I moved a little closer. "I don't need pills, baby. I can do it myself. I'll be ready real soon. Trust me."

I recognized the voice and I didn't even hear my breathing. The man just continued masturbating. I followed his eyes to the screen where Christian, bare-chested, sat in a chair as two women kissed his chest and worked their way down. One of those women was definitely Bee. The other may or may not have been Millie.

I murmured, "Nick, it's Dean."

Nick looked over his shoulder, saw it was me and immediately crawled under the bed's scattered covers.

With a child's whine, Nick said, "What the hell are you doing in here?"

"I'm looking for Millie. Have you seen her?"

Nick stuck his hands under the bed, gripped a remote control and turned off the VCR. A rerun of *The Nick Shaw Show* was playing on cable. Then he said to me, "Hey, that was one of our better shows, you know."

"Nick, don't fuck with me. Do you know where Millie is? I need to find her."

"She's with that Christian guy, Dean. The guy's all into her. Says she has a serious sensual mind."

I approached the bed. My face must have looked bananas, 'cause he cowered. "Shaw, where the fuck is Millie?"

In an amped-up rush, Nick babbled: "They left fifteen minutes ago. Said they needed some air. I think they just wanted some privacy. That's all I know, Dean. I'm sorry. It's been a real courtship, you know. Personally, I think it's time she gave him some."

Of course.

The roof.

Chapter 33

I exploded out of the bedroom door and dove into the revelers as if I was swimming against the tide. I saw Tanya, no longer dirty dancing, but being kissed by her two new pals. I kept pushing through. I saw Evander with his hands on both of Pamlesha's butt cheeks and her grinding up against his prone body. I kept pushing. I saw Tony, talking to two other tall men, point me out to them and laugh. I pushed my way out the door.

In the hallway, a few scattered dancers and seducers moved out of my way as I ran past. Must have been the look in my eyes. At the elevator I pressed the "Up" button like a fidgety game show contestant. Both elevators were on the ground floor. I counted to thirty and then, zoom, I was charging toward the staircase, kicking the door open, then taking them two at a time. I took out what was in my waist and held it in my hand so it didn't fall out. It was one of those plastic jobs, so it wasn't too heavy. Carrying it in my hand made me run faster.

At the sixtieth floor I grabbed my stomach, wiped my brow and then kicked the hell out of the "Exit" door. A gust of moist wind greeted me and I sucked it in as I got my bearings. In front of me was nothing but the Manhattan skyline. My ears filled with the sound of far-off traffic and my own frantic breathing.

Then, slowly, like a mosquito's low buzz, I heard two voices—both as breathless as me but infinitely happier. Frightened and fascinated, I turned and walked in baby steps around the stairway structure. It wasn't about sound anymore. I was being led by my nose. I could smell them. I could smell the fucking. I came around the corner of the stairway structure and saw a man's ass. His pants were around his ankles and his knees were bent, showing his powerful hamstrings. Christian pumped away at a woman whose legs surrounded his waist. The woman's head dangled over the side of the building. I couldn't see her face—just her strong legs. Her panting filled my ears. "Oh, Christian!" she shouted suddenly. "You're so good! Oh, Christian!"

The gun was in my hands and I aimed it right at the crack of his ass. I was gonna put a cap right through both their damn loins. It would have been easy. But it wouldn't have been me. I dropped the gun. After all my running and my anger and the sex I'd engaged in and the sex I'd seen, there was nothing left in me. I'd chased. I'd cheated. I'd been tricked. I was being cuckolded. Now I just fell to my knees with my face in my hands.

I'd been heading toward this moment for a while. I was almost relieved that it had come. I was like a piece of old china—cracked and finally coming apart. I heard someone walk over to me. I felt the person stand over me in judgment. "Dean?" It was a woman's voice. "Dean? It's alright, baby." I looked up and there was Millie, fully clothed, looking like a deity as she stood over me. There was a video camera in her hand.

I mouthed her name, not really making a sound, 'cause what do you say to a miracle? Over at the ledge, Christian was putting his pants back on and a woman was adjusting her hair. She looked at me and waved. It was Bee, looking as cheerful as a child.

I bent back down and closed my eyes.

"Dean?" Millie leaned down close to me, her hand touching my shoulder. "What were you gonna do with that gun?"

I opened my eyes and looked into hers. "I was gonna shoot you and your lover Christian right through his ass."

"Dean!"

"Dean, what? You don't call back. You don't talk to me. I got angry, baby, 'cause I love you. Do you understand?"

"Don't be mad at her, Dean." Bee stood facing me, her clothes zipped and buttoned back into place. Her face was strange—plaintive and satisfied, worried and sexy. "She loves you too."

"Excuse me," Millie responded in a catty voice I didn't know she possessed. "I don't need you to explain me to Dean."

"You sure about that, Millie."

"Bee, please!" Professor Christian Lawson walked over with a bottle of Kristal in one hand and three glasses clutched in the other. "This is not our business. We settled our issues—they have to settle theirs."

I stood up and stared daggers at this man whose pants were still unbuckled, shirt wrinkled and forehead wet with perspiration. The gun was at my feet. As he stood in front of me, my eyes dropped down toward it. Blood rushed to my head and, again, vengeance and jealousy filled my heart. I hated this man and I thought he needed to die.

Millie must have felt the heat of violence emanating from me, because she picked up the gun and thrust it toward Bee. "This must be yours."

"It is."

"Well, take it then." Millie slapped the gun into Bee's palm and then sucked her teeth. It was the most ghetto I'd ever seen Millie act and, to my surprise, it kinda turned me on. Christian—the controller, the manipulator—looked at me and there was fear in his eyes. It must have just hit him how close he'd come to death. Just one more moment of anger on my part— anger not undercut by grief and pain—and his ass would have been knocked right onto Columbus Avenue. His voice, so deep, so dark, was unsteady when he said, "Bee, let's give them some space, okay?" He took her hand and they walked away.

I was watching his back when Millie said, "Come with me, Dean," and guided me in the opposite direction until we stood by the ledge. We were silent at first. Where to start? The sound of a champagne cork being popped across the roof. I turned and saw Christian pouring the bubbly into two glasses Bee held. Once the glasses were clinked together in celebration, Bee and Christian sipped their drinks with practiced style and looked lovingly into each other's eyes. Christian turned away from Bee and looked over at us. "You guys want some?" he inquired.

Millie and I still stood quietly, our eyes full of the city's lights and our heads filled with things to say. Millie told him, "Give us a minute," and he went back to Bee, the champagne and his view of Manhattan. Millie still had that dress on from earlier in the night, so many lifetimes ago. I rubbed it with one hand even as she chastised me.

"You lied to me, Dean," she was saying. "You didn't tell me about Bee when you could have. It would have hurt—it did hurt when I saw Christian's footage—but at least you would have been honest, at least I'd know you had some truth in you."

"Truth?" I said quickly. "What about you and Christian?"

"You don't get it yet, do you, Dean? You don't understand me yet."

"What is it that I'm not getting?"

Millie held up the video camera. "I'm a voyeur, Dean. I like to watch people having sex, though not my boyfriend having it with another woman." I cringed but she continued.

"I also like to write dirty e-mails. But the only person I've slept with since meeting you is you." She paused a moment and let that sink in. "Sure, Christian has tried. He's a man. A very sexy one, in fact." She looked over at him with a leer that scared me. She saw how it affected me and shifted gears. "And you did sleep with his wife. But, unlike you, I make my own decisions about my body. I control who gets to touch it and who I touch. It's too bad you can't do the same."

"Millie, I love you. I want to marry you."

"But," she countered forcefully, "you don't understand yourself and you don't understand me." Again she looked over at Lawson and Bee. "I wish we were more like them."

"You mean crazy and freaky?"

"Dean, they are comfortable with who they are—whatever we want to call it. Besides, aren't we freaks too? I mean, why else would we be up here with them?"

"Good point," I said reluctantly, then pleaded, "Millie, let's go there together."

"I don't know, Dean."

"I do. I know you love me. I know I love you. If we can come together after all this, I know we can make anything we decide together work. I know it now."

Bee and Christian came over. He held the champagne and glasses. "What next?" she said to Millie. "You know he loves you?"

"So he keeps telling me," Millie replied.

"And she loves you too," Lawson said. "But, I should add, that love hasn't always worked for us. Sometimes it doesn't address all the problems."

Bee took Lawson's hand and looked at him. "Well," she said quietly, "it's never over, is it?"

"Seems not," he told her. Then he looked my way. "I'm sorry about whatever stress I've caused you. Whatever I did, I did out of love for Bee. Just like you ran up here with that gun out of love for Millie. I guess it just proves that we men are pretty silly."

"I guess," I answered. I was still getting this strange yet real set of relationships straight. "I think you better apologize or talk with or duck Evander. He didn't appreciate that baseball bat."

Lawson looked concerned and said, "He is a tough man. I snuck up on him. He definitely wants revenge."

"Don't anyone worry about Evander," Bee said. "I have Pamlesha with him. That'll cool any man down. No one is getting hurt tonight. Besides, we have some other business to handle." She leaned over toward me. "Your friend Nick Shaw is interested in having me audition for the cohosting job."

"That's nice," I said with a laugh. "But he's not having a very good time at the party. It might affect his judgment."

"Well, Christian and I are gonna go down and help him with his little problem. Are you coming down?"

"We need to talk some more." It was Millie. "We'll be down soon."

Christian left the open champagne and two glasses behind. They walked away hand in hand toward the stairway structure. Now it was just Millie, me and New York City.

"Do you want to make love to me up here, Dean?" She took my head in her hands and poured her eyes into mine. "I know it's your deepest fantasy. I want to be part of that, Dean. If we're gonna be together I have to know everything going on inside your dirty little head. No more lies. No more secrets. If it makes you happy—it satisfies something inside you—tell me. I'll make it happen—not Bee, not Christian—me, your lover, your wife. So, what do you wanna do now?"

"No, Millie, that roof shit is over. I've found a new fantasy and it's very simple. We can do it right now."

"What is it?" she whispered.

"I just want you to hold me. Hold me real tight for a long time. Like the rest of my stupid life."

"Your life isn't stupid, Dean. But you can be. You can be so stupid."

I bent down and rested my head on Millie's shoulder. She reached around me and drew me in. I felt like a child. The lights of Manhattan twinkled and shined, and then I closed my eyes.

Chapter 34

To the relief of leather salesmen, Con Edison and even the city's most ardent sun worshippers, fall finally arrived in New York the last week of October. As the longest Indian summer on record ended, the Knicks stumbled and bumbled out of the starting gate, agitating to no end my row mates David and Rashad. I only gave them the sketchiest outline of my tumultuous summer. They knew the wedding was on, that my Bee thing was over and that I'd squeezed all the freak out of my libido for a good long while.

Which was funny since on the night before Halloween, Millie and I ended up back at the scene of the deceptions. Bee's apartment—excuse me, Tony's apartment—was done up differently. Still rust-colored, of course, but in the center of that sunken living room a large circular dining table had been set up. Red candles were strategically placed for illumination but not to disturb the oh-so-important sight lines. In the candlelight the champagne glasses, the diamonds (the brightest of which resided in Tony's watch) and the eyes of the lovely couples, all twinkled.

Tanya sat next to Tony, who sat next to Kate, who sat next to

Evander, who sat next to Bee, who was next to Christian, who was next to Pamlesha, who was next to Nick, who was next to Millie, who was by my side. The meal, I was told, was Tony's idea, but as the Thai food courses came, one delightful platter after another, I got the distinct impression I was again working under Bee's direction. In fact, if you'd told me that there were hidden cameras aimed at the table (perhaps from behind those grasping rebounders?), I would not have blinked an eye.

Actually I hadn't wanted to come but Millie had insisted. She felt it was a bit of a test, a way to judge "where we are now." We'd been making all the right moves—narrowing down the choice of churches to two, finding a black caterer we liked, and writing (and editing) a long list of invited guests. Yet things were, not surprisingly, different between us. Millie had become more assertive in every aspect of our relationship. In bed she could be bossy—critical of me, but definitely mindful of what she wanted and needed. In social settings she was more likely to disagree with me than she had been before. Even when we were alone, an edge would sometimes appear in her voice. Instead of firing back, I'd often agree with her, just to get along. Felt like I was always being tested and, well, who could blame her? If I was to marry her, I knew that's how it was going to be. I was cool with that now. My number one job was not at *The Nick Shaw Show*—it was making this nice girl from Denver happy. Which is why we were sitting here with this strange crew of diners.

The talk at the table had been about what else? No, not sex. Media. The Professor pontificated on the role of HBO in "the visualization of our soft-core dreams." Shaw spoke of "opening up the dialogue on broadcast television, so it can compete with cable." Bee argued that "there is no longer any gap between our public and private selves, and all the media—new or old—does is reflect that fact."

Me? Mostly I kept my mouth filled with pad thai, nodded a lot and played with Millie's yoga-tightened thighs. I made a note to get Tanya researching a segment on yoga and sexuality. That old tantric thing everyone talks about and no one understands.

I was sipping on my third Thai iced tea when Christian kissed Bee with husbandly tenderness and then turned to his left, looked Pamlesha in the eyes, and then leaned over and slithered a lizard's tongue into her willing mouth.

"Oh," Millie said softly.

"That's your friend," I replied.

"He's a very playful man" was her disturbing response. I looked over at her and got nervous.

Tony, I guess being a gracious host, wrapped one long arm around Bee and the other around Kate and cradled them in his arms like two sweet brown babies, somehow creating a three-way kiss that curled my ten toes.

"Dean," Millie said. "Dean."

"Yeah."

"You're breathing heavy, Dean."

"Well, uh, I'm sorry."

"It's alright, Dean. Just be yourself. We're all friends here, right?"

All around the table kissing and pawing and fondling were accompanied by pleased sighs. The only person not involved, save Millie and me, was my boss, who sat staring at Tony's trio with happily envious eyes.

"Well," Millie said.

"Well," I answered.

"What do you wanna do, Dean?"

"Well. I know you don't mind just watching."

"You've learned something," she said with a warm grin.

"Yeah, it seems like it."

"So," she said, turning to stare at me, "you know what I could easily do. What is it that you wanna do?"

"You know, Millie. You have to know. If this is some test you concocted with them, forget me failing. I'm not failing. You hear me?"

Millie, ignoring the writhing, the clothes being pulled off and the rising tide of moans, stood up. She took my hand.

"We'd better go, then," she said, and I did as I was told.

FROM: SEECEE@HOTMAIL.COM
TO: ALADY27@EARTHLINK.NET
SUBJECT: THE PARTY

Sorry you left the dinner early. As you might have noticed, dessert was very special. That was not planned. It was Tony's party. We were just a very combustible collection, I guess. In lieu of your participation, I've attached some video footage. This is not intended as any violation of your renewed engagement. I see that you and Dean are good together. I would never again interfere with that relationship. I also know, from years of experience, that old habits die very hard. Once a voyeur, always a voyeur. We were destined not to be physical lovers. I see that now. My jealousy drove me to do some very obnoxious things. I've already apologized about that. One, however, can never be sorry enough for doing wrong. Perhaps we can resume our old relationship. I'll send you stuff. You watch it. We talk about how it made you feel. I used to enjoy corrupting you. You enjoyed being corrupted.

The choice is yours.

FROM: ALADY27@EARTHLINK.NET
TO: SEECEE@HOTMAIL.COM
SUBJECT: THE PARTY

The footage was wonderful. You and Bee were quite something together. I hope you two can keep it together. I know I'm working very hard with Dean. You can't believe the stuff he's now revealing about his childhood to me—it's like we've come back together at a deeper level. It's like sunshine after the rain.

I haven't told Dean about your e-mail yet.

For the time being, let's keep it to ourselves. OK?